CAST OF CHARACTERS

FAMILY SECRETS

*Five extraordinary siblings. One dangerous past.
Unlimited potential.*

Gideon Faulkner—The Coalition robbed him of his life. Now he wants to be free and discover the power of love, with whatever time he has left....

Brooke Carter—The small-town waitress finds herself swept away by a beautiful stranger—but is her mystery man the answer to her dreams, or a nightmare in disguise?

Jake Ingram—He's done it—he's found all of his genetically engineered genius siblings—but will it cost him his own life?

Agnes Payne and Oliver Grimble—Their evil plan is beginning to crumble, but they won't give up without a fight to the finish....

And don't miss the thrilling conclusion
to the FAMILY SECRETS series:
Check Mate by Beverly Barton, on sale May 2004

About the Author

INGRID WEAVER

admits to being a sucker for old movies and books that can make her cry. A RITA® Award winner for Romantic Suspense, she felt privileged to participate in the FAMILY SECRETS project with such a talented group of authors. And she was thrilled at the opportunity to tell the story of Gideon Faulkner, the mysterious criminal mastermind known as Achilles.

"When I write, I always tend to become involved with my characters," Ingrid says. "But writing *The Insider* was an especially moving experience. The obstacles that Gideon and Brooke had to overcome were enormous, yet the depth of their love for each other touched my heart. By the end of the book, I think I had fallen a little in love with Gideon myself."

Ingrid lives with her husband and son and a shamefully spoiled cat in a pocket of country paradise an afternoon's drive from Toronto. She invites you to visit her Web site at www.ingridweaver.com.

INGRID WEAVER

THE INSIDER

Published by Silhouette Books

America's Publisher of Contemporary Romance

Special thanks and acknowledgment are given
to Ingrid Weaver for her contribution
to the FAMILY SECRETS series.

SILHOUETTE BOOKS

ISBN 0-373-61378-4

THE INSIDER

Visit Silhouette at www.eHarlequin.com

Printed in U.S.A.

FAMILY SECRETS

Henry Bloomfield (d.) m. Violet Vaughn 2nd m. Dale Hobson

Susannah Hobson
m.
Travis Dean

Extraordinary Five

Connor Quinn
m.
Alyssa Fielding

Jake Ingram

Gretchen Wagner m. Kurt Miller

Marcus Evans m. Samantha Barnes

Faith Martin m. Luke Winston

Gideon Faulkner

"Uncle" Oliver Grimble m. "Aunt" Agnes Payne

Ingram Family

Clayton Ingram m. Carolyn Cook

Zach Ingram
m.
Maisy Dalton

Evans Family

Russell (Russ) Evans
m.
Lynn Van Allen

Charles Evans
m.
Sarah Alexander

Seth Evans

Laura Evans

Holt Evans

Drew Evans

Honey Evans
m.
Maxwell Strong

Birth Family
Adoptive Family
m.   Married
d.   Deceased

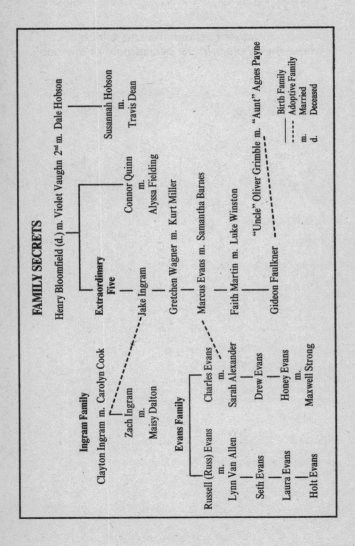

To James Hetfield and Lars Ulrich,
whose music plays in the background of this book.

Prologue

The crowbar slipped, striking sparks from the rock and ripping the leather that covered Gideon's knuckles. The door hadn't been opened since the tunnel had been sealed two decades ago. The damp air inside the mountain had corroded the hinges and cemented the bolt in place. The mechanism no longer worked as it was designed to.

Like him. He was as rusty as this forgotten escape hatch. Frozen in place. Self-destructing from within. Unseen, unknown…

"Get a grip," he muttered, his voice rumbling back from the rock that surrounded him. He repositioned the crowbar. "You're not even out yet and already you're losing it."

Iron scraped against steel. Gideon tested the strength of the lock, but there was no give to the metal. He played his flashlight around the edges of the doorframe, searching for a weak spot where the assembly was bolted to the tunnel wall. The crowbar was a primitive tool, but that and a chisel were all he'd been able to acquire undetected. He could have made explosives, but he wouldn't have been able to use them. Although he was too far from the inhabited areas of the compound for the noise of a blast to be heard, the seismic sensors around the perimeter would pick up the shock wave and someone would be sent to investigate the tunnel.

Gideon wasn't sure what he'd do if they found him. Could he take a life in order to preserve his own? How deep did the evil run in his soul?

Then again, only humans had souls.

And Gideon Faulkner wasn't quite human.

He checked that the rip in his glove hadn't reached his skin, then tightened his grip on the crowbar. Why was he doing this? He was safe here. He was valued. His sprawling quarters were furnished with every luxury that struck his fancy. He had so much wealth he'd needed to design a special program to count it. He had everything….

Except the truth.

He shook his head. That was ironic. Why would a man at the top of the FBI's Most Wanted list care about truth?

He turned to look behind him. The path through the mountain was swallowed by darkness, but he'd memorized every turn when he'd studied the schematic. The airlock that separated his quarters from the rest of the compound emerged too close to a public corridor to risk using, so it had taken weeks of painstaking labor to break through his bedroom wall to this tunnel. Once he had, it had been child's play to disable the alarm system—after all, he'd been in his teens when he'd invented it. The system was meant to keep intruders from getting in.

A person would have to be crazy to break out.

Crazy? Gideon's mind was his greatest asset, yet

would he know when he crossed the brink into insanity? It wasn't too late to go back to the compound. For more than twenty years it had been his sanctuary, the only home he'd known. Leaving the safety of his quarters, even for one night, could kill him. The vision that he chased could be an illusion. All he had were fragmented memories of a house by the sea. Dreams of a better place...and a different self.

What if there was no truth out there?

Or worse, what if he didn't like what he found?

With a growl like the warning of a trapped animal, Gideon pushed aside his doubts and swung the crowbar at the door. Vibrations shot up his arms and rattled his teeth. He widened his stance, his muscles bunching, and swung again.

A chunk of rock flew back from the edge of the doorframe. Three more broke loose with the next blow. Gideon jammed the end of the crowbar into the gap and threw his full weight against it.

Metal screeched. Rock crumbled. The bolts that held the doorframe to the tunnel wall snapped. Gideon jumped backward as the door crashed to the floor at his feet.

Dust billowed in a choking cloud. He shielded his face with his arms and held his breath until it settled, then cautiously moved forward. When he filled his lungs once more, he tasted something strange. Something different. A fresh, sharp tang like the soap he used, like the wooden shelves in his library when they had been new.

It took him a heartbeat to realize what he breathed. It was fresh air.

Damn, he'd done it. He was out.

Gideon grabbed his flashlight and propped the door into place behind him. He had six hours left before he'd be missed. That should be enough time to cover the three miles to town and begin the search for the truth behind his memories. According to the topographical maps, cutting across country would be rough in places until he could parallel the highway, but as long as he didn't encounter something unforeseen—

A monster loomed in front of him, so tall it blocked the sky. Gideon lurched back, directing his flashlight beam upward. Limbs swayed in the darkness, trailing fragrant tendrils through the mist. A tree. He recognized it from the pictures he'd studied. It was a hemlock, part of the pocket of old-growth forest surrounding the buildings that concealed the compound.

He reached for a branch and ran his gloved fingers along flat needles slick with mist. He moved deeper into its shadow, his boots slipping on hillocks of moss. His nostrils flared as rich, earthy scents swirled around him. He pressed his hand to the trunk. Through a protective barrier of supple kidskin, he explored the contours of the bark.

It was dangerous to linger. Precious minutes were passing. This was only a hemlock tree, after all. Nothing special.

He closed his eyes, his senses whirling. Nothing special? Damn, it wasn't a photo in a book or an image on a screen, it was a *real tree.* And for the first time in his life he was touching one, smelling one, hearing the branches sigh in the breeze....

Or was it the first time?

Something danced on the fringe of his consciousness. He felt air on his face, but it wasn't laden with the scents of the forest; it was tinged with salt. The breeze became the crash of waves. Sunshine warmed his skin—

The vision winked out as soon as he reached for it. Gideon pushed away from the tree and began his journey.

One

The man was crossing the empty parking lot when Brooke first saw him. In the glow of the Christmas lights that ringed the front window, his black-clad form was etched with red, making him seem like some demonic apparition against the brooding darkness of the Oregon forest.

She hesitated, her hand on the Open sign that hung in the restaurant door. It must be fatigue that was making her fanciful. This guy was no apparition, he was probably some down-on-his-luck logger waiting for a ride. The Highway Grill was a regular stopping place for truckers who drove the route through Redemption. Hitchhikers weren't uncommon, but traffic had been sparse tonight. The pulp mill had cut back to one shift, and the town's other major employers had closed for the holidays. If the stranger in the parking lot was waiting for a rig to pull in, he might be out of luck.

The mist that had cloaked the town all evening had given way to fine snow only moments ago. Brooke had hoped to lock up early, but if that man wanted to wait inside where it was warm, she couldn't very well turn him away. Instead of flipping over the sign to Closed, she let it swing back into place against the glass.

He tipped up his face as he moved into the pool of light from the lamp over the restaurant's entrance. Snowflakes swirled downward to settle on his forehead and his cheeks, turning his skin moist where they melted. He ran his tongue slowly over his lips, as if savoring the taste of the snow.

The action was unexpectedly sensual. Brooke's pulse thudded in a mindless response.

But he was licking *snow,* for God's sake. Was he that thirsty, or was he simply nuts?

He drew off his gloves and stretched out his hands. The shoulders and sleeves of his black coat were becoming dusted with white, as was his hair, but he didn't appear to notice. His entire being seemed to be focused on watching the snowflakes melt on his palms.

The location of the restaurant hadn't concerned Brooke before. In fact, she found its isolation on the edge of a small town reassuring—Frank would never find her here. Aside from the occasional passes she'd had to fend off from overeager customers, in four years Brooke hadn't encountered any trouble more serious than a few drunks who had refused to pay their bill or a bear that had wandered down from the mountain to rummage through the garbage out back.

But her final customer had left ten minutes ago. Cheryl, the other waitress, was visiting her family in Des Moines until after the holidays and Mabel, the grill's owner, had taken the night off to attend the Christmas pageant at her grandchildren's school. The only person within shouting distance was a man who was behaving as if he'd never seen snow before.

Brooke was reaching for the dead bolt, about to reconsider her decision to keep the grill open, when the man turned toward the door. Through the glass and the swirling snow, his eyes met hers.

Oh, God. How could she have been afraid of him? He had the gaze of a lost child. Someone left behind. His eyes were filled with a loneliness so deep and aching that Brooke withdrew her hand from the lock and held it out to him before she realized what she was doing.

The man's gaze shuttered instantly. Whatever she'd thought she'd seen there was submerged beneath a carefully blank expression. He put on his gloves and watched her warily.

Brooke dropped her hand and backed away to let him enter, embarrassed by her impulsive gesture. What had come over her? She must be more fatigued than she'd thought. The loneliness of a lost child? Maybe he should be the one who should be worried about being alone with her.

The man waited until she had taken several steps back before he pushed open the door. He paused on the threshold as the bell over the doorframe tinkled. Looking up, he moved inside and let the door swing shut. He watched intently as the overhead hinge set the bell into motion once more, as if he found the simple device fascinating.

Brooke rubbed her palms over her apron and headed for the counter. This was getting weird. She searched for something neutral to say in an attempt to establish some normalcy. "The snow shouldn't last."

He glanced down at his coat. "Yes, it's melting already."

His voice was deep, filling the room as easily as his presence. His boots thudded against the linoleum as he moved past the booths that lined the front wall. He ran the tips of his gloved fingers over the surface of the varnished pine tables, his gaze darting everywhere.

How could she have thought there was anything childlike about him? He was all man, from the musky evergreen scent he'd brought inside with him to his fluid, athlete's stride. He was at least six feet tall. His shoulders were broad, but he didn't appear bulky. Brooke guessed that his body was as lean and hard as his face. "I meant the snow outside," she said. "According to the radio, they're not predicting any accumulation."

He cocked his head and listened. A country tune played softly from the speakers mounted on the wall.

"Are you waiting for a ride?" she asked.

"Is that what you're doing?"

"No, I thought you were."

"Do you work in this place?"

His questions weren't really odd, she thought. They followed logically from her responses, but they seemed out of step somehow. "Yes. Would you like a coffee?" She put the counter between them and gestured toward the round glass case that sat in the middle. "We close at midnight, but there's still enough time if you'd like a piece of pie, too. We have blueberry, mincemeat and chocolate cream. Fresh baked this morning."

He walked to the opposite end of the counter from where she stood and regarded the three-tier pie keeper in grave silence, as if choosing a piece of pie were a life-or-death decision.

Now that she could see him more clearly, she realized he couldn't be a logger as she'd first assumed. His overcoat was fine wool and had the look of expensive tailoring. The leather gloves that encased his hands likely cost more than her new winter parka. His complexion wasn't ruddy enough for someone who worked in the outdoors. His hair was thick and black, combed starkly away from his forehead and tied with a band at the nape of his neck.

She imagined his hair would brush his shoulders in lush abandon if it was released. As a rule, Brooke didn't care for long hair on a man, but it suited this one. Give him a head scarf and a gold stud in his ear and he could have walked off the deck of a pirate ship.

A pirate who licked snow? Oh, for heaven's sake. Her imagination was getting out of hand. Plenty of men wore their hair like that. She'd seen more than a few ponytails on some of the research scientists who worked at the town's two high tech companies...

Of course. That would explain everything. His smooth skin, his good-quality clothes and his eccentric behavior would be perfectly normal for a scientist who worked in a lab all day. Those guys didn't get out much.

Still, this one must get as far as a gym, considering the way he moved. *Prowled* would be a better word. With each step he emitted the controlled strength of a large predator testing the confines of its cage.

She emptied the coffeepot into a mug and pushed it toward him. ''Go ahead, it's on the house.''

He studied the mug the same way he'd regarded the pie but made no move to approach. "No, thanks, I don't have time. I only came in to ask for directions."

"Which way are you headed? Up the highway to Redcom or into town to Taber?"

He lifted an eyebrow. "That's very astute reasoning. How did you reach your conclusion?"

She gave him a smile. "Elementary, my dear Watson. You look like someone who makes his living with his brain, not his hands, so you're probably on your way to one of those research facilities with all the computers. Are you new in town?"

"Yes, this is my first time here. I'm looking for Taber Aviation."

"I thought they were closed for the holidays."

"Someone will be there. Can you direct me to it? The map I studied appears to be out-of-date."

"That's not surprising. The town's been working at straightening the highway for months. My boss calls it Redemption's make-work project. It makes jobs for the road crew and boosts the local economy because of all the lost travelers who wind up here." She pointed out the window to show him what she meant. "Ignore the detour signs and follow the old road around the bend to the pulp mill. Go about a quarter mile, take the first road on the right after that and you can't miss it. Taber has a jet engine mounted on the lawn out front."

"Thank you."

She focused on the empty parking lot. "I didn't see your car. Did it break down? If you need to call for a tow truck or a taxi, there's a pay phone beside the door.''

''Thank you, but that won't be necessary. I'm... enjoying the walk.''

She returned her gaze to him. He probably was staying in one of the fancy houses at the base of the mountain. These days, only the high-tech scientists could afford them.

He turned as if to leave, then looked at her over his shoulder. ''Why did you call me Watson?''

''Sherlock Holmes.''

''That's not my name, either.''

She laughed, assuming he was joking. When he continued to regard her without joining in, she realized she'd made a mistake. ''I was referring to the books by Sir Arthur Conan Doyle.''

''I'm not familiar with his works.''

''Holmes was a detective who liked to reason problems through logically and Watson was his sidekick.''

The corners of his mouth lifted in a slow smile. ''Ah.''

His smile was as subtly sensual as a whisper of velvet. The sound he made was a rumble of pleasure, setting off a wave of renewed awareness. Brooke's pulse thumped the same way it had when she'd seen him lick his lips.

It jarred her. He was a stranger. It was closing time and she was tired. Why was he affecting her this way? She had turned down offers from men who were better looking than he was. Not that he was hard to look at, but his features were too harsh to be called handsome. And besides, he wasn't making her any offers, was he? He'd been careful to keep at least ten feet of space between them since he'd walked in the door. He didn't even want a piece of her pie.

She picked up the coffee he'd declined and poured it from the mug into a foam cup, then snapped a plastic lid on top and carried it around the counter. "Here," she said, closing the gap between them. "One for the road. If you don't drink it, you can warm your hands on it."

He appeared to hold his breath as he stared at the cup in her hand. Finally, he clenched his jaw and reached out. His gloved fingers brushed hers as he took the cup.

The warmth of the leather surprised her, as did its texture. It was as supple as silk, sliding over her skin in a delicate caress. The contact was tantalizingly brief, over almost as soon as it started.

He exhaled as he backed away. "Thank you."

Whatever casual response she might have given him died on her lips. The careful blankness he'd kept on his face since he'd walked in the door had slipped. The shutters over his expression had parted and the loneliness once more shone through.

It hadn't been an illusion. It was as real as the leather that had touched her knuckles. He was studying her as if he wanted to feel her warmth on his hands the way he'd felt the cold of the snow.

As if he wanted to run his tongue over her and learn how she tasted.

She could feel his need. It rose like pheromones in the air around them. Not just sexual desire, but a longing for human contact that was more basic than sex and beyond the scope of words. Its power stunned her. Who was this man? *What* was he?

Gideon took another step back, the woman blurring before his eyes. The familiar vision arose in his consciousness. He could smell the sea. He could feel sand grit between his toes. The warmth that bathed him was from more than the sun, it was from…kindness.

But he'd never known kindness, had he? How could he recognize it? The Coalition valued strength. Kindness was a weakness. It made you vulnerable to attack.

Yet the warmth drew him. He strained toward it. There had to be more. *Please, let this be real, too…*.

The cup slipped from Gideon's fingers and hit the floor, yanking him back to reality. He leapt backward before the hot liquid could splash his legs. His boots skidded, sending him crashing into a table. It dragged a chair over as it fell.

He'd gone for weeks without seeing anything, but tonight it had happened twice. The first time had been because of the tree. This time the woman had triggered it. Her smile, her decency. The sweet torment of her flesh-and-blood presence. Damn, if she knew—

"Are you okay?" She started around the toppled furniture and stretched out her hand.

Gideon backed away before she could get too close. "Yes. I'm sorry. I…" He was accustomed to lies, but he rebelled at the thought of lying to her.

Yet what could he say that would sound sane? Could he tell her that he'd glimpsed a piece of his past, or what he hoped was his past? Would she help him if he told her he longed to glimpse it again? "I slipped," he said. "I'll clean this up."

She glanced at her hand and let it drop to her side. She leaned down to right the chair. "No, I think you should sit down while I get the mop."

He watched her as she hurried toward a swinging door behind the counter. She wore a white apron over her denim skirt. The ends were tied in a bow at the small of her back and swung in rhythm with the movement of her hips. Her sweater was the deep green of the moss he'd seen beneath the trees and had an intricate texture his palms itched to explore. Her hair was a mass of soft curls tumbling down her back in the colors of autumn, a laughing tangle of red, brown and gold. He'd had no more than a whiff of her scent when she'd leaned close to him. It was as pure and light as snowflakes swirling from the darkness.

He picked up the empty cup and righted the table, then splayed his hands over the smooth wood top and fought to steady his thoughts. He was on overload. Too many inputs to process at once. He'd known that leaving the compound would be difficult, but he'd badly underestimated the extent of the challenge.

Everything was *real*. Theory was suddenly practice. His books hadn't prepared him for this. More details bombarded him with each minute that passed.

She returned carrying a bucket and mop. Her cheeks were flushed. "It's just as well it spilled, since it probably would have killed you, anyway."

He straightened up fast. "What?"

"The coffee. It must have been sitting on the burner for an hour and could have eaten its way through that cup on its own."

She was joking again. She did that to cover up her discomfort, he realized.

But she had been right. If she had touched the rim of the cup or breathed on the fluid inside it, the coffee would have killed him.

She set the bucket on the floor. Her forehead furrowed. "Please, I really think you shouldn't be on your feet. You didn't look too well a minute ago."

Gideon soaked up her concern as greedily as he'd absorbed her kindness. "Contrary to how it must seem, I haven't felt better in years."

She shook her head. "Fatigue can sneak up on you. Believe me, I know. It causes all kinds of strange effects. Have you been on the road for long?"

"It's difficult to judge the time when each experience is so…involving."

"I've never heard it put quite that way before," she said.

He needed to make more of an effort to appear normal. But how the hell could he do that when he'd never had a casual conversation? He had confrontations, not dialogue. How was he supposed to deal with someone who didn't want anything from him?

And how could he pretend every nerve in his body wasn't aware of each breath she drew? The reality of her presence, her actual living presence, was intoxicating.

She watched him for a moment before she turned to her work. She used a device with rollers that was fastened on the side of the bucket to wring the excess moisture from the mop, then passed the mop over the floor.

Gideon focused on what she was doing. For his own safety, he was never present when the maintenance crew cleaned the various sections of his quarters so he hadn't taken an interest in how it was done. The combination of mop and wringer was as ingeniously simple an innovation as the bell over the door. He took a deep breath and moved close enough so that he could curl his fingers around the mop handle. He tugged the mop from her grip. "Please, let me."

This time she was the one to back away. "You don't have to do that, Watson. I was going to wipe the floor after I close up anyway so—"

"Gideon," he said.

"What?"

"My name is Gideon." He cleaned the last of the coffee from the floor. He noticed a trail of melted snow that he must have carried in on his boots and wiped that up, too. "I apologize for my clumsiness."

"Don't worry about it."

"It was a poor way to repay your kindness, Brooke."

"How do you know my name?"

He returned the mop to the bucket and gestured toward her left breast. A small metal pin engraved with her name was fastened to the front of her apron. "Elementary, my dear Sherlock."

She smiled.

Gideon focused on her lips. The warmth that spread through him wasn't from a vision this time.

Her name suited her. He'd seen a brook in the forest during his hike from the compound to the road. The edges had been locked in ice, yet in the center the water had sparkled and chuckled as it rushed over a path of smooth stones. It had been a feast for his senses, but not as rich as this woman with her cascade of autumn hair and the compassion in her eyes.

How would she look at him if she knew what he was?

Two

"I hope they lock him up and throw away the key when they catch him." Mabel MacKenzie, the owner of the Highway Grill, settled her reading glasses more firmly on her nose and snapped her newspaper indignantly. "It's been almost nine months since that Achilles bastard fleeced the World Bank and my portfolio has just started to recover."

Brooke had to step around Mabel's stool to reach the oven. As usual, Mabel was sitting in the center of the restaurant kitchen to take advantage of the strong light from the fixture over the work table. Brooke suspected Mabel needed a new prescription for her glasses but was too stubborn to admit it. "You shouldn't read the business section so early in the morning," Brooke said, taking the last pie from the oven. "It's bad for your blood pressure."

"It's not the business section, it's the front page. The FBI claim they're closing in on him." Mabel leaned over to slap the paper on the table. A cloud of flour puffed upward. She waved it away and pointed to an article in the lower left corner. "It's about bloody time. My taxes pay their salaries, but they've been running around like a bunch of Keystone Kops since April. I don't know who's the bigger thief, Achilles or the government.''

Brooke set the pie on the cooling rack beside the others, put down the pot holders and paused to skim the article. Even after all this time, the World Bank heist still made the front pages. The amount the man known as Achilles had stolen was too huge to grasp. At more than three hundred fifty billion, the number of zeros involved boggled Brooke's mind. The crime itself had been executed electronically through a complicated series of computer frauds that the authorities were still trying to unravel. No one had been physically hurt. Unfortunately, the aftereffects that had rippled through the economy were still causing a different kind of pain.

Pension funds had collapsed overnight when the stock markets had crashed from the widespread investor panic in the wake of the robbery. Businesses had failed from a lack of investors. Mabel had lost most of her life savings and wouldn't have been able to keep the Highway Grill open if Brooke hadn't offered to take a cut in wages, in exchange for free use of the restaurant kitchen in the off hours to run her own business.

Brooke had always dreamed of establishing a bakery, but her plans had been postponed. The money she'd saved—and the financing she'd arranged—had been wiped out when the Redemption Savings and Loan had failed last spring. By running her custom-order pastry business from the grill's kitchen, she hoped to build her customer base and recover some of the money she'd lost.

So far, the effort was beginning to pay off. The tough economic times seemed to have made the small indulgence of Brooke's pastries more in demand than ever. She leaned over to scan the paper. "This article doesn't give any new details," she said.

"You're right," Mabel muttered, snatching the paper back. "It's probably government propaganda. A little crumb of hope that's meant to keep the rabble from rioting. Bunch of incompetent fools. If I ran my restaurant the way they ran the country, I'd be broke in a week."

Brooke swept the pieces of leftover pie dough into a pile and regarded Mabel fondly. From the day Brooke had arrived at the Highway Grill, Mabel had been more of a friend than an employer. She had accepted Brooke's offer to work in exchange for a meal, had let her bunk down in the back room for the night and hadn't asked any questions as she'd fixed an ice pack for her bruises. Mabel freely admitted to being opinionated, vain and stubborn. Displays of affection embarrassed her, and she got prickly and demanding when her arthritis flared up. How could Brooke help but love her?

Mabel clicked her tongue impatiently as she brushed away the film of flour that had coated her fuchsia skirt. She had remarkably shapely legs for a woman of sixty-two, a fact of which she was fully aware, and she displayed them today in sheer black stockings. Her spike heels were three inches high and matched her suit. Her white hair was cut in a short, no-nonsense style that accentuated her sharp cheekbones. Her teeth were large, strong and whiter than her hair, and when she smiled she looked more like a wolf than someone's grandmother.

"What are you smirking about?" she demanded.

Brooke grinned. "Just thinking about how great you look. I wish I was thin enough to wear a suit like that. Did you have a good time at the Christmas pageant?"

"You're trying to change the subject when I haven't even gotten warmed up. I was about to treat you to one of my rants."

"Taxes, the government or Achilles?"

"I'm in a mood to do all of the above. The damp weather is hell on my joints." Heaving a sigh, Mabel folded the paper and recrossed her legs. "The pageant was great. Sherry was an angel and Jonathan played one of the lambs in the field. They both were brilliant."

"Naturally. They're your grandchildren. Do you have any pictures?"

She hooked the toe of one fuchsia shoe into the strap of the purse she'd dropped beside her stool and swung it up so she could grab it. "I thought you might ask. I put some Polaroids in the zippered pocket on the side. Oh, wait until you see Sherry's wings."

Brooke wiped her hands on a towel as she went to stand beside Mabel. The photos were full of excited children and harried parents. The economic fallout from the World Bank heist had made for lean times in Redemption—and there wouldn't be many gifts under most Christmas trees—but the town was recovering, just like the rest of the country.

"Thanks for holding down the fort last night so I could attend," Mabel said. She returned the snapshots to her purse and slid from the stool. "How was everything here?"

"Fine. Quiet."

"I figured it would be. Did you close up early?"

"Almost."

"These smell good," Mabel said, pausing to sniff the pies. "I love mincemeat but it gives me indigestion."

"I'm doing eggnog tarts tomorrow. You'll like those."

"I'll also need an elastic waistband. What do you mean that you *almost* closed early?"

"A man came in to ask for directions when it started to snow. He, uh, was here until midnight."

Mabel snickered. "A *man* asking for directions? That must have been weird."

"Oh, it was weird, all right."

Mabel's expression sobered. She tipped her head and peered over her glasses at Brooke. "What happened?"

"Nothing, really. I was tired, so he probably seemed odder than he was."

"Brooke, there's odd and then there's odd. You should have called Trevor if you didn't like the situation. He would have been here in a flash."

"It wasn't a police matter, so I had no reason to call him."

"Trevor would take any excuse to drop by, Brooke. He wouldn't care whether it was official business or not. You know that."

"Yes, I know that. Everyone in town knows that."

"You could do worse."

"I already did," Brooke pointed out.

"It's been four years, Brooke. Not all men are like Frank."

"My final customer wasn't, either, so, like I said, there was no reason to push the panic button." Brooke turned back to the table to continue cleaning up. "The guy was just on his way to Taber Aviation. All those scientists are a bit weird."

"Hmph."

Brooke clapped her hands to her cheeks. "Oh, my God, Mabel. You sounded just like my neighbor's grandmother! She always makes that noise, too."

"Grandmother, my ass. You're trying to get me mad so you can change the subject again."

Mabel was right, Brooke thought. She was changing the subject because she didn't want to talk about Trevor or Gideon. She was sorry now that she'd mentioned the stranger of the night before.

On the surface, her encounter with Gideon hadn't been out of the ordinary at all. She'd told him how to get to Taber, he'd spilled some coffee and then had helped to clean it up. And then he'd left.

She didn't want to tell Mabel how she'd watched him until he'd disappeared around the bend in the highway, or how she'd looked for him while she'd driven home and thought about him until she'd fallen asleep and awakened to a dream of him this morning.

His loneliness haunted her. It might be melodramatic to put it that way, but there it was. Fatigue or no fatigue, she knew what she'd seen and what she'd felt. The whole time they'd been having their ordinary encounter, there had been something happening beneath the surface. There was so much more to Gideon than met the eye.

Mabel squeezed Brooke's shoulder. "Take tonight off. You've been getting up at dawn to fill all those holiday orders. Then you work a full day for me. That's too much."

"No, thanks, I'm fine. With Cheryl away, we're shorthanded already." *And Gideon might come back.*

The eagerness that accompanied the thought startled her. She didn't try to deny it, though. She was never much good at hiding her feelings.

Years of practice at hiding his feelings allowed Gideon to keep his face expressionless as he turned toward the camera in the bedroom ceiling. He matched his position to the image that would be on the loop of video he'd programmed to run through the night, then counted down the seconds until the live feed would take over.

He stretched slowly, as if he were luxuriating in the slide of the satin sheets on his skin. Right on cue, music wafted from the speakers in the wall. He'd chosen Chopin for today, a mournful interpretation of a nocturne. For a moment he lay still and listened, as if gathering the energy to get up. In reality, he was trying to calm his heart rate.

He'd had no sleep. The six hours he'd allowed himself were almost up when he'd returned to the mouth of the tunnel. He'd worked quickly to reset the alarms as he'd wound his way back through the mountain, but it had taken longer than he'd anticipated to reach his quarters.

It wasn't due to a miscalculation of the time. It was because he'd been drunk on sensation, high on the sheer number of new things he'd experienced on the outside and reluctant to return.

But he'd had no choice. Not if he wanted to continue living.

He rolled to the edge of the mattress and sat up. His movement triggered the lights. They strengthened slowly, allowing him time to verify that the black velvet bed-hangings behind his bed were back in place so they hid the plastic sheeting that sealed the access to the tunnel. The carpet under his bare feet was hand-knotted wool, an intricate geometrical design of black and gold sculpted on a deep burgundy background. He flexed his toes over a ridge in the weave, checking for any telltale dust as he stretched his arm to pick up his silk robe.

"Good morning, Gideon."

It was Agnes Payne's voice, rasping through the speakers over the Chopin. She and her husband, Oliver Grimble, were the closest thing to parents Gideon had. They had been in charge of his health and his education during his youth, and for a time he'd had the misguided hope that they actually were his parents, but Agnes had set him straight. Neither she nor Oliver had provided the genetic material from which he was created.

He'd had donors, not parents. He was a scientific experiment, the product of gene manipulation, conceived in a test tube thirty-three years ago during Code Proteus, a CIA project funded by the government.

In essence, he wasn't fully human. That was why

he didn't remember his childhood. His earliest memory was of waking up in a room packed with medical equipment, his mind hazy from drugs, his body in agony. He'd been ten years old, and he'd barely survived the emergency surgery that had been required to remove a bullet from his heart.

He still bore the scar from the wound, a souvenir of the night the government had ordered Code Proteus terminated.

Gideon pulled on the robe and fastened the belt, more to give himself time to think than to shield his nudity. He had no self-consciousness about his body. He'd learned early on the only privacy worth guarding was the privacy of his thoughts.

The cameras in his quarters were supposedly for his protection; in the event of a medical emergency, the continuous monitoring would ensure that someone could be suited up and dispatched through the airlock to administer aid. As a youth, he'd taken the surveillance for granted, since it was the only life he'd known. Later he'd grown to understand that the monitoring had another purpose.

As long as the Coalition was able to watch him, they felt secure that he was within their control. He'd never given them any reason to doubt his loyalty. Why should he? They had saved his life when the government had tried to kill him. They gave him the modified food and isolated environment that kept his body alive, and they provided the intellectual stimulation that fed his mind.

Essentially, the Coalition was as vital to his continued existence as he was to theirs. It was a delicate balance that neither side dared to upset.

He ran his fingers through the fringe that flowed from the silk at the ends of the belt. This was what Agnes would expect. A lazily decadent motion, typical of the self-indulgent persona it had been convenient for him to adopt.

Not that he didn't enjoy his luxuries. Considering the limits of his life here, he craved the sensual stimulation he found in his quarters.

But that was before he'd discovered that all the luxuries money could buy couldn't compare to the soft kiss of snow on his tongue. "Hello, Agnes," he said, feigning a yawn. "You're up early today. Is something wrong?"

"I was about to ask you that, Gideon."

He continued to finger the silk fringe and forced his breathing to remain steady. They couldn't know about his nighttime excursion. He'd left his clothes and his muddy footware in the tunnel. Should he have returned his gloves and overcoat to the cold room in the lab? No, he had other coats there. The absence of one wouldn't have been noted. It was only his guilty conscience making him think—

Guilty conscience? Hell, he couldn't afford to go there. He had sufficient sins to feed his guilt without adding his deception of Agnes to the tally. "Damn right, there's something wrong, Agnes. What happened to the Renoir I asked for? The painting should have been delivered last week."

"We have it. There's been a delay with the decontamination procedure. The age of the canvas precludes our usual heat treatment. We want to be absolutely certain it's safe to bring in.''

''Who is responsible for the delay?'' he demanded.

''Many of our staff wanted to go home for Christmas so we're shorthanded. I will take care of it personally, Gideon. I promise.''

''When?''

''As soon as possible. By next week at the latest.''

He rose to his feet. ''Good. I look forward to it.''

''As I look forward to learning the details of your new project.''

He almost faltered then. *Could* she know? The sole reason he'd risked going outside was so that they wouldn't be able to detect what he was doing. That was why he'd gone to Taber Aviation—their computers had allowed him to access distant databases without being monitored by the Coalition. Searching for the truth about his first ten years would be viewed as a sentimental weakness to Agnes, unnecessary and unprofitable. Truth was a flexible commodity with the people of his world. It would be dangerous if they discovered that he was questioning the version they had given him.

''Our plans are advancing, Gideon,'' Agnes said. ''We need those additional funds soon.''

She wasn't talking about his search into his missing years, he realized, she was talking about the next robbery.

Brooke had said he looked like a man who made his living with his brain instead of his hands. It was more than that. He was kept alive because of his brain. But right now he wanted to use his hands. He wanted to curl his fingers around that crowbar again and feel the satisfaction of unleashing his physical energy on a target other than a locked door.

Gideon heard something rip. He looked down. He had wrapped the belt of his robe around his fists so tightly he'd shredded the fabric.

"When shall I expect your first progress report?" Agnes asked.

He kept his face blank as he turned toward the camera. The best way to deal with the Coalition's demands was to make demands of his own. Greed was a language they understood, and Gideon had made sure to master it.

"When I have the Renoir on my library wall," he said.

There was a pause. "Agreed."

"And I've decided there's something else my library needs, Agnes."

"Yes?"

"The complete works of Sir Arthur Conan Doyle."

"Why?"

He lifted an eyebrow, as if the answer should be obvious. "Because I don't have them."

"Very well, I'll see what I can do. We'll talk again later."

The link terminated and the Chopin returned to drift languidly through the speakers. Gideon moved to his bathing area and dropped his robe. He opened the gold-plated faucets that controlled the flow of water to the shower and stepped into the marble-tiled room. A mist of water that had been warmed to the exact temperature he specified sprayed from eight separate spigots to massage his body.

He'd had this shower installed a year ago in exchange for the motion-sensitive scanning device he'd invented as part of a security system. The money the design had earned for the Coalition was perfectly legitimate, as were the billions his other inventions had brought in over the years.

But those funds fell far short of what the Coalition needed to finance their ambitions. Even the three hundred fifty billion he'd stolen from the World Bank last April wasn't enough for them. They wanted him to do it again. They wanted him to use his genetically enhanced intellect and his computer skills to pull off a robbery that would make the record-setting World Bank heist seem insignificant. This time he would simultaneously target every major stock exchange in the world.

He knew he was capable of doing it. That wasn't why he was stalling.

He adjusted the water to increase the flow and lifted his arms. Droplets needled his skin as he rotated within the spray. He grabbed the soap and lathered himself from his toes to his forehead, let the water punish his skin, then lathered again.

Yet even if he scrubbed until his skin was raw, he knew it wouldn't do any good. If he'd acquired any lethal contamination while he'd been outside these walls, this surface cleansing would be too little and too late to save him.

The same genetic alterations that had given him his superhuman intellect had left him with a fatal flaw—

in order to enhance his brain function, his DNA had been engineered so that he lacked the particular amino acid that inhibited synaptic response. Gamma-aminobutyric acid was present in every normal human being, but if Gideon was exposed to it, it would trigger the total shutdown of his body on the molecular level, an irreversible cascade of immune responses that would end with his death.

Still, as dangerous as his foray of the night before had been, he'd been as careful as possible. The only object from outside that he had consumed or had permitted to touch his bare skin had been crystallized distilled water. Snow. He'd touched nothing man-made without his gloves. The only person he'd seen had been Brooke, and he'd maintained a safe distance from her throughout their encounter. She'd held out her hand, twice, but it would have been suicide to pull off his gloves and risk direct contact. He hadn't even let himself breathe her air.

He'd wanted to. Damn, he'd wanted to breathe *her*. He'd been so alone for so long. What would it be like to feel someone else's skin against his, someone else's warmth?

He flattened his palms against the marble wall and dipped his head under the force of the water. His gaze fell on the puckered white scar that gleamed through the hair on his chest.

There were many ways in which Brooke's world could kill him.

Then why had being there made Gideon feel so alive?

* * *

The security system that had been installed at Taber Aviation was state-of-the-art. It was built around a device that was programmed to run random checks of the locks, the equipment and the motion sensors in the corridors. There were backup programs that ran checks of the primary program; there were storage batteries at various locations throughout the building in case of a power interruption. There was even a gyroscope at the heart of the main board that would keep the system functioning through a moderate earthquake, so most of the high-tech companies on the quake-prone west coast had already installed the system or had one on order.

It was one of Gideon's more profitable designs.

Gideon entered the building through the side door and swiftly disabled the alarm. He hadn't encountered any trouble when he'd been here yesterday—the holiday shutdown had left the place practically deserted—but he couldn't permit himself to become complacent. He would find a different computer to use this time and allow himself ninety minutes, no more. That should be sufficient time to make progress…as long as he stayed focused.

Would he ever get used to it, this onslaught of sensation? Even in this utilitarian structure made of concrete and glass, there was a dizzying number of things to discover. There was the sound his boots made on the tightly woven carpet, the looping patterns of shadow the overhead lights left on the walls, new smells, new ideas….

He pulled off his leather gloves and replaced them with a pair made of surgical latex as he walked down the ground floor corridor. The high-tech facility was kept spotlessly clean and dust-free, but it wasn't germs that concerned him. What he needed to avoid was much smaller and more subtle, the trace residues left by human contact.

He bypassed the labs where the prototype designs would be constructed—the security there was tighter and would be more difficult to breach—and turned toward the administration offices. After choosing a door at random, he pressed a slim magnetic device to the handle, a useful burglary tool he'd designed for the Coalition. Seconds later, the tumblers clicked in the electronic lock and Gideon walked inside.

His pulse was elevated, pounding in his ears the same way it had when Brooke had smiled, yet unlike then, it wasn't pleasant. He was nervous. Inside his gloves his palms were sweating. This was another new sensation for him. He'd masterminded countless crimes, but until yesterday he'd never done any hands-on before.

The rush of adrenaline wasn't logical. Breaking and entering was inconsequential compared to his other deeds.

He closed the door behind him, scanned the room and went directly to the computer that sat on a long, low table behind a desk. Minutes later, he had booted up, made a few adjustments to the hard drive that would mask his use of the terminal and logged on to the Taber server.

He'd run across the first newspaper story on the Internet by accident. He'd been searching the media for information about the World Bank heist, verifying that the authorities were continuing to chase the false trails he'd laid for them. He'd been checking for rumors about Achilles. Instead, he'd found something else.

The scandal sheets had been filled with the story, and it had been met with understandable skepticism. There had been headlines like Mutants Among Us and CIA Supermen. The articles about genetically engineered babies and secret government projects had the same level of credibility as the reports of alien abduction and Elvis sightings.

But then he'd found the same story in the reputable *Washington Post:*

Recently declassified documents reveal the existence of a secret government program to breed a superior human being. Over three decades ago, when the science of genetics was still in its infancy, researchers in this country had already broken the genetic code. Their aim was to create physically perfect individuals with enhanced intellectual capabilities.

The facts had agreed with what the Coalition had told Gideon about his origins. Except for one detail.

Using CIA funds and secret gene-manipulation techniques, the scientists of the Code Proteus project successfully bred five individuals....

Five. *Five.* He'd been told he was unique, and he'd seen no evidence to contradict that. Yet if the Coalition had lied to him about that fact, what else had they lied about? What if he wasn't as alone as he believed? He could have brothers and sisters somewhere who had been forced to live in hiding like him. Where were they now? Did they share his genetic flaw? Would they understand what he'd become in order to stay alive? Or had they been terminated by the government along with the experiment?

Could they tell him about the house by the sea, and the person he'd been before he'd become Achilles? A better place and a different self. He had to know if it was true, and he had to know before he committed his next crime.

Perhaps it was futile to hope the evil inside him wasn't complete, that one less crime would make any difference. If it weren't for the lives he read about in his books, he wouldn't have known that goodness existed.

He didn't waste any time with the newspaper archives—he'd memorized everything he'd found yesterday. There had been plenty of speculation but there had been no new facts. Someone had slammed the lid back down on Code Proteus. That wasn't surprising. The government agents who'd tried to have him killed wouldn't want those facts made public.

So Gideon went where the public couldn't. He accessed the CIA mainframe first, but Code Proteus had been disbanded twenty-three years ago, when electronic data storage wasn't as routine as it was now. He found names, but no files to go with them; funding approvals, but no details of the research.

The lid had been slammed down here, too. He

memorized the information he found, but it was sparse. Far less than he'd hoped.

Oddly enough, he'd had more luck piercing the blank wall of his past during the few minutes he'd spent with Brooke.

Three

After a week of watching for Gideon's return, Brooke had almost convinced herself he wouldn't be coming back. The well-educated, well-paid people who worked at the town's high-tech companies didn't often frequent the Highway Grill. Their type would prefer the more sophisticated restaurants in town that catered to the Taber and Redcom crowd and served fancy plates with tiny bits of low-calorie food arranged like artwork.

So when she backed out of the kitchen two days after Christmas, balancing a pair of turkey platter dinners with extra gravy and side orders of onion rings in her hands, and turned around to see him sitting on a stool at the opposite end of the counter, she could almost attribute the spike in her pulse to surprise.

She didn't, though. Her reaction was from interest, not surprise. He was as intriguing as she remembered. His hair gleamed like liquid midnight from its pirate queue. His tall, broad-shouldered form dominated the space around him. He had his hands in his coat pockets and his gaze on the chalkboard where Mabel had listed the specials. It was a seemingly casual pose, yet Brooke felt if she moved close enough she'd be able to hear his senses hum like a high-tension wire.

"Brooke, honey, hurry up. I'm dying over here."

She crossed the floor to the booth in front of the window. It was half an hour before closing time, so there were only two customers remaining. She set the platters on the table and summoned her best professional smile for the middle-aged man who had spoken. "Paul, you could hibernate for the winter on what you've got stored up under that vest. I'm surprised you could fit in any more turkey."

His companion laughed and slapped his hand on the table. "She got you there, Paul."

"She can get me anytime, Phil. The woman knows the quickest way to a man's heart is through his stomach. When are you going to marry me, Brooke?"

Brooke rolled her eyes, well accustomed to Paul's meaningless flirtations. "And break the hearts of every waitress from Eugene to Cheyenne? I couldn't do that. Besides, you're not a big enough tipper."

He grinned and ran his hand through his white hair. "Nag, nag, nag. It's like we're married already."

"Could you fill my thermos, Brooke?"

"Sure, Phil," she said, turning to the second man. "I made the coffee extra strong, just the way you like it. It'll eat the rust off your rig."

The men chuckled at what was an old joke and turned their attention to their food. Paul and Phil were two of the truckers who were regulars at the Highway Grill. They did the route through Redemption every few weeks or so. They were running late tonight, though, so with no further delay Brooke gathered the thermos bottles the men had left on the table and carried them back to the counter.

Gideon had moved his gaze from the chalkboard to a salt shaker. His black overcoat was unbuttoned, revealing a snug black turtleneck sweater. He was turning the chunky container in his fingers and watching the salt crystals flow against the glass. He was wearing gloves again. They were black and probably expensive—the leather was supple enough to show the outline of his knuckles and the shifting tendons on the backs of his hands.

He had large hands, Brooke noticed, yet he manipulated the salt shaker with delicate, refined motions, like someone accustomed to doing precision work.

Would his touch be gentle like that with a woman? Or would the need for contact that she'd seen in him be too strong for gentleness?

"Hello, Brooke."

His voice was as deep and rich as she remembered. She looked from his hands to his face to find him studying her. "Hi, Gideon. How's the new job at Taber going?"

He seemed to ponder the question for a moment. "The work I'm doing at Taber is going well, thank you. How are things going with you?"

"Fine, thanks. I'll be with you as soon as I fill these bottles." She grabbed the coffee pot from the heating ring, reminding herself of her own job. "Think you might risk a piece of pie tonight?"

"Thanks, but no."

"I swear I haven't lost a customer yet."

"I'm sure they're very good, but I wouldn't want to ruin your perfect record. I...have to be careful what I consume."

"You mean you have allergies?"

"Something like that."

"Oh. What a shame." She finished filling the first bottle and screwed on the lid. "People come from miles around for my pies."

"Do you make them yourself?" he asked, a strange note in his voice. It was more than surprise; it was as if he hadn't realized *anyone* could actually make a pie.

"Pies, rolls, eclairs, anything sinful and decadent."

A corner of his mouth lifted. "You have a novel interpretation of decadence, Brooke."

At the sight of his half smile, her pulse spiked again. She took the second thermos and heaped several spoonfuls of sugar into it. "Waitressing is my day job," she said. "But it's my dream to own a bakery. I pretty well grew up in one."

"Do you have good memories of your childhood?"

It hadn't taken long for the conversation to get odd. She glanced across the room and saw that Paul was wiping gravy from his plate with a chunk of meat and Phil was smothering his onion rings with ketchup. There was a clatter from the direction of the kitchen— no doubt Mabel had decided to rearrange the storage cupboard Brooke had organized that morning. Brooke wasn't alone with Gideon this time.

Yet she felt as if he were drawing her into the aura of solitude that surrounded him. She considered Gideon's question. "Times were tough when I was a kid, but the bulk of my memories are good ones. Like most people, I've probably blocked out the bad."

He looked thoughtful. "What are some of your good memories, Brooke?"

''The smell of fresh-baked bread,'' she said immediately. ''That warm, yeasty smell that makes you feel as if you've walked into a hug.''

He stared at her in silence, as if he had no idea what she was talking about.

She laughed self-consciously. ''My mother and I lived in an apartment above the bakery where she worked. She would go downstairs and start on the bread before dawn to have it ready for when the shop opened, so that's the smell I woke up to each morning. I loved it.''

''Perhaps you dream of opening a bakery because you're seeking to recapture the vision from your childhood.''

That threw her. She'd thought she was simply being practical by wanting to start up her own business, and baking was a skill she excelled at. Yet there was truth in what Gideon had said. Maybe she was hoping to rebuild the good parts of the life she'd left behind.

Well, she'd already figured out that he was bright. She set down the thermos and gave her full attention to Gideon. ''Okay, it's your turn now. Tell me one of your good memories.''

He lifted the salt shaker in his hand. ''Sand between my toes. A breeze that tastes of salt.''

''That sounds lovely. Tell me more.''

He lifted a shoulder. ''I don't remember much about my childhood. Perhaps I've blocked it out. Whose music is that?'' he asked.

''What?''

''The melody that's playing from the speakers. I don't recognize it.''

She realized he wanted to change the subject. Although she was curious, she let him; she wouldn't want anyone to stir the memories she had blocked out either. She paused to listen to the radio. "That's an old song by Alabama."

"The state?"

She smiled. "The group. Mabel's the country music fan, so that's why the radio's glued to this station."

"Mabel?"

"My boss," she said, tipping her head toward the back room. "Also the grill's owner and chief cook. She's been trying to convert me to country but I prefer soft rock. What about you?"

"If I had to state a preference, it would be Beethoven."

That figured, she thought. "I don't know much about highbrow music."

"All you need to know is how to listen. Then you can hear Mozart's humor or Chopin's delicate melancholy. Handel's work sings with power, Bach's with mathematical order."

"I always thought it was stuffy, but you make it sound fascinating."

"It is. The appeal of music is universal and takes no special ability to enjoy. Every culture in the world, no matter how primitive, has some form of music."

"You're right. That's interesting."

"Even more interesting when you consider that of all possible things we can create, music serves no practical purpose other than to feed the soul."

Definitely a weird conversation, but she was enjoying it. She leaned her elbows on the counter and propped her chin in her hands. "So what flavor is Beethoven?"

"Passion. Torment." He looked at her. "Rage."

"Is that why he's your favorite?"

"Possibly."

She could see something stirring in the depths of his eyes. It was dark, almost…evil. She had a sudden flash of the way he'd first appeared to her, tinged in demonic red.

She shook off the feeling. Gideon might be mysterious, but he had exhibited nothing except gentleness. Although he looked like a pirate, he spoke like a poet. And then there was his loneliness. She couldn't forget that.

He returned his gaze to the salt shaker. "There is music in the sound of the waves," he said. "It has a rhythm as if the sea is breathing. It runs and laughs across the sand like children."

Like a poet, she thought again. Brooke waited for him to continue. When he remained silent, she prodded quietly, "Children?"

The leather over his knuckles tightened as he gripped the shaker. "There are children."

"Where?"

"They're playing on the sand."

His voice had lowered. It was barely above a whisper. His eyes lost focus, as if he stared through thick glass at something too distant to measure. It was the same way he'd looked the other time, just before he'd dropped the coffee cup.

She moved closer, concerned. "Gideon?"

"Gideon, let's go. Race you to the house."

The boy's voice was so near, Gideon knew if he turned around he would see who was speaking. He felt a shadow move across his back as he knelt on the wet sand. He swung his head from side to side. He didn't want to go in yet. He'd made a water-wheel generator that would recharge the batteries of his toy truck and he had to wait for the tide to come in so he could test it.

"Hey, Gideon. What did you make this time?"

Another voice, this time a girl's. A second shadow flickered over the sand as a wave lapped the edge of the channel Gideon had dug. The wheel started to turn.

"Everyone, come and see what Gideon built. This is cool!"

More shadows clustered around him. He watched the wheel pick up speed. It turned the series of gears that led to a copper coil that would develop the electric field. The needle of the gauge in the side began to move, just as Gideon had calculated. He smiled.

"Gideon? Are you okay?"

The vision faded gradually. The sound of the sea melded into the twang of a guitar and a man singing about a truck. There was the clink of cutlery against dinnerware. The sunlight dimmed to yellow overhead lamps that hung from the ceiling. He wasn't kneeling in wet sand, he was sitting on a stool padded with vinyl. Brooke stood on the other side of the counter, the skin of her forehead furrowed into lines of concern.

He felt an unfamiliar tension in his cheeks and realized he was still smiling, just as he had in his memory. He focused on Brooke and his smile grew. "I'm fine," he murmured. "Thank you."

She tilted her head to peer at him more closely. "You sure? You looked as if you drifted off for a minute there."

"I was just...remembering." He marveled to himself as he said the words. The memory had come so easily this time, and it had been more detailed than ever before. Gideon was certain it was genuine. He still felt an echo of the pride his younger self had felt over his water-wheel generator. And he could still hear the echo of the children's voices.

Children. He hadn't been by himself on that beach. Were the others who had called to him his siblings? They would have to be. Otherwise they wouldn't have been able to stand so close to him safely.

His smile faded. Agnes had told him that he'd been raised alone indoors in a lab because he couldn't risk the contamination of the human world. She and Oliver had said his days had been structured around the special learning programs they had developed for him. He'd had no playmates. His only outside contact had been the scientists who had monitored his progress.

Obviously, they must have lied.

That confirmed what he'd expected. This was why he'd chosen to leave the compound in order to find the truth. And it was a good thing that he'd stopped regarding Agnes and Oliver as his parents long ago. Otherwise, learning they had lied about his past might have hurt.

But Gideon wouldn't let it hurt. After all, he wasn't quite human enough for that.

"This time of year makes me sentimental, too," Brooke said. "It's natural to get lost in the memories sometimes."

He returned his attention to Brooke. "Why?"

"Christmas and all. Did you celebrate with your family?"

He hesitated, trying to think of a way to answer without lying. Life in the Coalition compound didn't make allowances for special occasions like Christmas. Often the traditional holidays were their busiest times, since many institutions were short-staffed and security was lax. After all, that was why he'd chosen this week to make his excursions to Taber Aviation. "I had to work," he said finally. "What about you?"

"I made dessert for Mabel and her family, so they had to let me stay for dinner." Before she could say more, the bell over the door tinkled. Gideon looked around to see who had entered the restaurant.

A large man in a sheepskin jacket stood to one side of the door. His feet were braced apart, his weight held forward as he scanned the room. He appeared to be near the same age as the two diners—truck drivers, Gideon assumed from their rigs parked outside—but his posture was far less relaxed. His body language announced authority. So did the gold badge that gleamed from his lapel.

Police. Just a local cop from the looks of him, Gideon thought. It would be pointless to run. Not only would that draw unnecessary attention to himself, he had no reason to fear being recognized. Every law-enforcement agency in the world was after Achilles, yet no one knew what he looked like. No one had seen his face except the top people in the Coalition.

And of course, Brooke too.

With a casualness he did not feel, Gideon looked away and picked up the plastic-coated menu folder that was wedged between a sugar jar and a napkin dispenser. Logically, he had nothing to fear, but he'd been told so often of the fate that awaited him should he ever fall into the hands of the authorities, he couldn't prevent the hard twist in his gut.

"Evening, Brooke," the cop said, striding toward the counter. He swung his leg over the stool in front of the glass pie keeper and unbuttoned his jacket. "Give me a piece of that mincemeat pie, would you? It's been a long shift."

"Sure, Trevor. In a minute."

Gideon glanced at her and nodded to the menu he held. "Go ahead. I'll wait."

Although she kept her smile on her face as she moved to serve the new arrival, she didn't look pleased at the interruption, Gideon thought. Was it because the man was a cop, or because of the man himself?

The man's gaze flicked from Brooke to Gideon. Gideon recognized the look. He'd seen enough territorial posturing among the members of the Coalition to understand when he was being warned away from an object of interest. This man was interested in Brooke.

Ordinarily, Gideon didn't back down from a challenge. He couldn't. The Coalition was quick to capitalize on any weakness. Yet in this case, it would be senseless to respond. Brooke interested him. Oh, yes. The mere sight of her through the window had drawn him inside tonight. Yet all he could do was look. He could never possess. Gideon flipped to the next page of the menu and pretended to be absorbed in the prices of the various sized beverages.

"This is terrific, Brooke," Trevor mumbled around his first bite of pie. "Really great. As good as my mother used to make."

"Thanks."

"All the way back from Portland I was thinking about this." His fork scraped against his plate as he continued to eat. "And you, too," he added. "You look pretty tonight. Is that a new sweater?"

"Yes, Mabel's daughter gave it to me for Christmas. She knitted presents for everyone this year. What were you doing in Portland?"

"Official business. The FBI wanted to meet with representatives from all the local forces."

"Really? What's going on?"

Trevor scraped the plate clean. "Can't tell you. Like I said, it's official business. I'll have another one of these, Brooke," he said, pushing the plate toward her. "And could you get me a large milk, please?"

As Brooke refilled his plate there was the scrape of boots from the other side of the room. At the edge of his vision Gideon saw the two truckers approach the cash register. "How are the roads, Sheriff?" the white-haired man called out.

"They're clear," Trevor replied. "But if you're heading out now, better watch for black ice. The temperature's supposed to drop ten degrees by morning."

"Sure thing. Thanks, Sheriff. Brooke, have you got our coffee?"

Gideon kept his movements slow and easy as he closed the menu and replaced it behind the napkin dispenser. He took advantage of the activity as the truckers paid their bill to ease off his stool and move to the exit.

It was still just as pointless to run, but it was definitely time to leave. What had brought the FBI to Portland, and why did they want to meet with the local police? Gideon believed he knew the answer. The real question was what was he prepared to do about it.

The temperature had already begun to drop as the sheriff had said. Gideon buttoned his coat to his chin and flipped up his collar as he crossed the parking lot. Instead of continuing toward town and to Taber Aviation as he'd intended, he headed back the way he had come. He followed a path parallel to the highway, keeping to the edge of the forest. After two miles, he could see the glow from the floodlights that illuminated the turnoff for Redcom Systems.

As one of Redemption's two high-tech employers, Redcom brought a welcome boost to the local economy, particularly now that the environmentalists had essentially halted the logging of the old-growth forests. While Taber specialized in aviation research, Redcom manufactured communication and security devices for clients around the world. The company was well-respected and extremely profitable. It also had computers that surpassed the facilities at Taber.

But not for one second had Gideon considered using the Redcom computers for his search into his past. He knew that the computers, the phone lines, every mode of communication that was installed at Redcom was monitored by the Coalition. Because, in fact, Redcom *was* the Coalition.

It was all very neat. The buildings that housed Redcom's research and manufacturing activities had been constructed to conceal the sprawling underground complex of the Coalition's hidden compound. The electrified fence and around-the-clock surveillance at the perimeter of the Redcom property were supposedly to guard against industrial espionage, just as the rigorous security checks visitors had to pass through were to ensure client confidentiality. Even the massive amounts of rock that had been excavated during the most recent expansion of the compound had been explained by Redcom's need to construct a solid foundation for the company's most delicate instruments.

The reputation of Redcom was beyond suspicion, and the Coalition took measures to keep it that way. They neither targeted nor ignored Redcom clients. They even employed legitimate scientists who knew nothing of the secrets they walked over each day, although the scientists were as much for camouflage as the building itself, for Gideon's inventions provided the bulk of Redcom's profits.

In effect, the world's leading supplier of security systems was run by thieves. For over twenty years, no one had guessed the truth.

Probably because the lie was so big.

Gideon headed into the forest before he could be spotted by the cameras at the turnoff. The going was slower here, but he'd become more adept at negotiating the slope over the past week. He reached the mouth of the tunnel several minutes later, put the door in place and reset the alarms as he walked deeper into the compound. As he had all week, he stripped down in the tunnel and left his clothes outside his bedroom wall. He had peeled back the plastic and was reaching for the velvet that concealed the hole when he heard the voice.

"Gideon? We need you to get up now."

Damn, he'd suspected this might happen. This was why he'd left the grill when he had and cut tonight's excursion short. Trevor wasn't the only one who would know the FBI were in the area. He flung the fabric aside and dove through the opening.

"Gideon. Wake up."

It was Oliver's voice. He sounded worried. Usually Oliver Grimble picked up his cues from his wife, and it took a lot to worry Agnes. Gideon snatched the controller he'd stored underneath his bed, hit the key that would end the video loop he'd programmed and slid between the sheets. He counted three seconds before he moved again.

Light slowly filled the room. Gideon rubbed his face and sat up.

"Good," Oliver said. "It's about time. We—"

"What the hell's going on?" Gideon cut in. He swung his head toward the clock. "It's not even one."

"I know, and I apologize."

Gideon started to rake his hair off his face, then realized his hair was still tied at the back of his neck. Damn, he could only hope that Oliver was too rattled to notice. He fell back on the pillow and laid his forearm over his eyes. "There's no activity scheduled tonight."

"This is an emergency. We're assembling in the main conference room."

"I need more sleep," he muttered. "You know I'm not to be disturbed during one of my scheduled rest periods."

"I apologize again, Gideon, but I really must insist."

He yawned and stacked his hands behind his head so he could work his hair loose with his fingers. "This had better be important, Oliver."

"It is. The meeting starts in five minutes."

"I'll be there in fifteen."

"Ten."

Gideon stretched and rolled to his side. "Agreed."

The main conference room of the Coalition was reserved for only top-level meetings. It was at the physical heart of the compound. Like the rest of the underground structure, it was shielded from any possible electronic eavesdropping by layers of concrete and lead sheeting. There were only two ways in. The first was through a private elevator that ran from the office of the president of Redcom Systems to the quarters Agnes and Oliver shared. The second was through the closed-circuit video system that was wired into Gideon's computer lab.

Gideon kept them waiting for more than a minute, then positioned his chair in the spot where he could comfortably view the monitors from all the conference-room cameras. Schooling his features to an expressionless mask, he punched the switch that would activate the link and bring his own image into the meeting.

The lights over the oval table in the center of the room were dim, not in deference to the hour but for dramatic effect. The leaders of the Coalition missed no opportunity to convey the impression of power. Against the shadowed background of the steel-riveted walls, the pools of illumination over each chair served as dramatic spotlights for the three people who were present.

At the head of the oval table was Willard Croft, the former CIA operative who had been the government liaison for the original Code Proteus team. He was a thin, balding man around sixty, with watery brown eyes and a smile that flickered with the frequency of a nervous twitch. Even at this hour, he wore his typical white shirt buttoned to his throat and the knot of his tie crammed tightly against his collar. He sat with his forearms on the edge of the table and his shoulders angled forward like an underfed bird of prey.

When Code Proteus had been terminated, Croft had helped Agnes and Oliver rescue Gideon, then had faked their deaths in a house fire and had brought them to safety in Oregon. Because of this, he'd had to give up his career and go underground himself. Gideon owed him his life and his loyalty, a fact Croft reminded him of on a regular basis.

"Thank you for finally joining us, Gideon," Croft said, turning to the screen where Gideon's image glowed. "Now that we are all present, we can get started."

Croft was taking charge of the meeting, as usual.

He liked to believe he was the guiding force of the Coalition, but the real power rested with the woman who sat to his left.

Gideon moved his gaze to Agnes Payne. Unlike Croft, she was sitting ramrod straight in her chair, probably in an attempt to make herself appear taller. She was a woman driven by ambition and the need to dominate. Physically, she was unremarkable. While she might have been attractive in her youth, years of bitterness over the way fate and the government establishment had ruined her life had honed her features to forbidding sharpness.

Looking at her now, Gideon felt a twinge of longing for the warmth he remembered in his vision. He thought about Brooke, and he wondered what fresh-baked bread smelled like.

Agnes acknowledged Gideon's presence with a casual nod, but her dark eyes flashed with impatience. "It took Oliver several minutes to rouse you, Gideon," she said. "Are you feeling unwell?"

He yanked his thoughts back on track. This wasn't the time for sentiment. These people would pounce on any sign of weakness. "You all know I don't like to be disturbed. This is the second time in one week. It's unacceptable."

"We're sorry, Gideon," Oliver said. "I know you're working hard at the new project, but this couldn't wait. We need to move up the timetable."

Gideon shifted his gaze to Oliver. The beam of light that shone on him was as bright as the light that spotlit the others, yet he seemed eclipsed by his wife. Of the three people at the table, he wielded the least power.

That didn't make him less dangerous. Under Agnes's influence, Oliver was as ruthless as any of the others.

"Impossible." Gideon folded his arms over his chest and leaned back in his chair. "I don't yet have my Renoir."

"Gideon, I told you I'd see to that matter personally," Agnes said.

"I bargained in good faith," he said. Of course, it was a lie. Even if they had managed to steal ten Renoirs for him, he would still be stalling.

Croft drummed his fingers on the table. His nails needed trimming; they sounded like talons. "We don't have time for your tantrums, Gideon. We've just learned the FBI are in Portland."

"Portland is one hundred and twenty-three point seven miles from here," Gideon said. "I imagine the FBI are in many other cities, too."

"Ingram is with them," Oliver put in.

Gideon lifted an eyebrow. "Jake Ingram, the special investigator hired by the World Bank?"

"Yes. That's why we have to move as soon as possible."

"Well, well, well. So he worked through the red herrings I put in his path. The game is getting interesting."

"Dammit, you freak, this isn't a game!"

At Croft's outburst, Gideon's expression hardened. "Freak?"

Croft wouldn't meet his gaze. "I meant—"

"My price just went up," Gideon said. "I want the Van Gogh sunflower study that sold at auction in New York last month."

"And you shall have it, Gideon," Agnes said crisply. "As soon as is humanly possible."

It was no accident that she stressed "humanly," Gideon thought. It was all part of the negotiations. He nodded, his point made.

"You must remember, we're all under stress," Agnes continued. "Willard more than the rest of us. It's hard for him to watch the government he once served and admired be overrun by those who want to kill us. You know better than any of us what lengths they will go to to ensure everyone who was connected with Code Proteus is dead."

Gideon remained silent. He'd heard this all before.

"That's right," Croft said. "I know how our government agencies work. We'll never live to go to trial. They'll assassinate us, just as they tried to eliminate you twenty-three years ago."

"We can go underground anywhere," Agnes said. "But it's you I'm worried about, Gideon. Our research into solving your genetic flaw isn't yet complete. All it would take is one unguarded moment, one careless action, one molecule of DNA from a normal human being and your body will turn on itself as your immune disorder manifests."

Gideon felt a sharp pain in his fist. He'd closed it so tightly it was cramping. He forced his fingers to relax one by one. He'd heard this all before, too. So many times. He knew in explicit detail each stage of his body's self-destruction should his disorder ever be triggered. It would be slow and excruciating and totally unstoppable.

Agnes swayed forward, speaking directly to the

camera. "Don't ever forget you can't eat or drink anything outside the safety of these walls, Gideon. You can't let anyone touch you. Only we can keep you alive. You must help us."

Gideon swore under his breath, the first outward sign of emotion he'd allowed. He knew she was right. If the police closed in, he had the most to lose. The sense of freedom he experienced when he slipped out at night was as elusive as his memories. Impossible to sustain or possess. Foolhardy to pursue.

"How soon will you have the programming ready?" Agnes asked.

Gideon inhaled slowly, buying time. Some part of him wanted to do what she asked. Damn, it was always so much easier to simply comply. He fought to hang on to his thoughts. He saw an opening and decided to gamble. "Before I give you an answer, I want you to answer something for me."

"Certainly. What is it?"

"What happened to the other children of Code Proteus?"

If he hadn't been watching for it, he wouldn't have seen it. The flicker of Agnes's left eyelid, the quick intake of breath. From the monitor on his right, he saw Croft draw back. Oliver made an involuntary sound that he covered with a cough.

Agnes was the first to recover. She broke the silence. "Why would you ask me that, Gideon?"

He kept his gaze steady on hers. He needed to tread cautiously or he'd stir their suspicions. "You're all so positive we're marked for assassination, even after twenty-three years, it makes me wonder. Why would the government be so anxious to kill everyone associated with Code Proteus unless the results of the experiment had been duplicated?''

She looked at Croft first, then at her husband. ''Perhaps it's time he knew the truth.''

Gideon felt a rush of surprise. Was she admitting she had lied? Could it be this easy?

Yet could he believe anything she said now?

''I'm sorry, Gideon,'' Agnes said. ''We thought it best if you didn't know. You're right. There were other successful breedings. Five others.''

Breedings. Not births, not children. He shouldn't let it hurt. ''What happened to them?''

''One was flawed and disposed of at birth. The others survived to adolescence but we couldn't reach them in time. The night you were shot, your mother—''

''My what?''

''Sorry, I mustn't put this in sentimental terms. It will only make it harder on you.'' She lifted her chin. ''I meant Violet Vaughn, the woman who was hired to carry the embryos during the experiment. She was fanatically dedicated to Code Proteus—that's why she allowed the government to use her reproductive system.''

Violet Vaughn. He'd seen that name in the CIA files, so Agnes was telling the truth about Vaughn's involvement in Code Proteus. But was she his mother?

No, he wasn't human enough to have a mother. He had a woman who had been paid for the use of her reproductive system. One of his siblings had been *dis-*

posed of at birth. He struggled to pull in his feelings, to suppress the horror. He couldn't show weakness.

"Vaughn was the only person who could slip past the security Oliver and I had installed on the lab," Agnes said. "That's why the government chose her to carry out their orders."

Something stirred in the depths of his mind. It wasn't a warm memory like the ones of sunshine on the beach. It was dark and painful. Panic. Fear. The scent of violets. The stench of gunpowder. A dark-haired woman wavered in his vision.

"Violet Vaughn shot the other four test subjects in their sleep, Gideon." Agnes's words tangled with the nightmare. "She believed ending your lives with a bullet would be more merciful than exposing all of you to gamma-aminobutyric acid and watching you die slowly. After successfully terminating the others, she left you for dead. You were almost gone when we found you bleeding on the floor of your bedroom."

Yes, the woman in his vision was looking at him, her blue eyes narrowed with purpose. He had been groggy from sleep and had tried to fight her off, but he was too small. He screamed for help, but she wouldn't leave him alone. Agony exploded in his chest and his white pajamas turned crimson—

Gideon hit the switch that would terminate the connection to the conference room. The monitors went black. He swiveled his chair to face away from the camera. He was breathing hard. Sweat beaded his upper lip and trickled coldly between his shoulder blades. The scar on his chest throbbed.

What if there was no truth out there?

Or worse, what if he didn't like what he found?

He closed his eyes to shut out the vision, unwilling to see any more.

Four

"That was a mistake, Agnes." Croft paced the shadows behind the table, his tread unusually heavy for such a thin man.

"No, it wasn't. We knew Gideon's conditioning would break down in time. He no longer responds to the hypnotic trigger we gave him in his childhood, so we have to find a way to manage any emerging memories."

"What do you mean? Doesn't that nursery rhyme work anymore?"

Agnes sucked on her teeth in irritation. "No. As I said, the hypnotic trigger is ineffectual."

"I thought the memory wipe you and Oliver did was total."

Oliver cleared his throat and twisted to keep Croft in sight. "Nothing about the brain is completely certain, Willard. Even in the case of severe brain injury where large areas of tissue are destroyed, some subjects develop new pathways along undamaged neurons and surpass all reasonable prognoses."

"Are you saying he's going to remember everything?"

"Given enough time, it's quite possible," Agnes said. "His question about his siblings could have been arrived at logically, but it could also suggest the process has already begun.''

''Son of a bitch.''

''Perhaps I should remind you that we're not dealing with an ordinary subject,'' Oliver added. ''A normal human brain would not have the ability to recover from the extreme treatment we administered, but because of the genetic alterations—''

''The freak is healing himself, is that it?'' Croft stopped behind his chair and curled his fingers over the back. ''You should have thought of that years ago.'' He looked from Oliver to Agnes. ''Can't you increase the amount of the psychotropic drugs in his food?''

''Yes, we'll try that tomorrow, but we must use caution,'' Agnes said. ''We've already exceeded what we calculated to be the maximum daily dosage, and we have to leave him with enough free will to form independent thoughts. Otherwise, he would not be able to exhibit creativity. We need his brain functioning or he will be useless to us.''

''How long before he remembers the truth?''

''That depends. I've suspected it has been happening for months. It appeared to have begun at the time of the World Bank heist. He's covered it well, but I've noticed him becoming less cooperative.''

''Why didn't you inform me?''

''It was irrelevant. We can't afford to confront Gideon at this point, Willard. Besides, I believe we can manipulate him by other means.''

Croft dropped into his chair. ''What other means?''

Agnes smiled. ''I already demonstrated it. Make

him afraid to stir those memories that are surfacing. Play on his sense of loyalty by reminding him how much he owes us. Focus his energy on resenting the government and fearing what will happen if he falls into their hands. In short, give him no choice but to obey us if he wants to live.''

Oliver pressed his fingers to his lips for a moment. ''I'm concerned that Gideon may be too strong-willed to be controlled by strictly psychological or emotional manipulation for long.''

''It was effective tonight,'' Agnes snapped. ''Didn't you see his expression before he terminated the video link?''

''Yes, but of all the children, he was the most difficult to control. He had a natural resistance to the drugs we used on the others. I would advise caution. If he ever realizes the truth—''

''By then it will no longer matter,'' Agnes said.

''But—''

''Dear, would you unlock the elevator?'' she interrupted. ''Victor is waiting upstairs to join us.''

''Victor? Surely the situation with Gideon isn't that unworkable.''

''I believe in tying up loose ends.''

Oliver frowned. Nevertheless, he moved to do her bidding, as he always did. He opened the control panel beside the elevator doors, punched in the combination to activate the mechanism and pressed his thumb to the scanner. When the light over the elevator glowed green, he turned to face his wife. ''Do you want Victor to deal with the FBI?''

''We must keep them from closing in until we've

moved to the next phase in our plan. The failure of our other agents to stop Jake Ingram before now is unfortunate, but this time there is no room for error."

"You're right," Croft said. "We are at a critical stage."

"Once Gideon gives us what we want by completing the plans for the next robbery, we will have enough funds to put our people into place around the world," Agnes said. "After that, Victor can take care of another loose end."

"Who?" Oliver asked.

Agnes glanced at him. "The work on the new compound in Arizona is almost finished. We never did include any separate quarters for Gideon there."

Croft laughed, a quick bark of noise. "That's right, we didn't."

Oliver wrinkled his brow, as if just realizing the oversight. "But where will we keep him?"

Agnes's eyes glittered. "Our research into Henry's notes is nearing completion as well. Once we succeed, we can breed an entire army of Gideons to do our bidding. He will have outlived his usefulness to us."

The elevator doors slid open soundlessly. Oliver started and took a step away.

The man who emerged seemed to bring a pool of stillness with him. Victor Prego was as gaunt as a skull. He looked around the room with the unhurried gaze of a carrion eater, calm, dark and oddly blank. His devotion to the Coalition was total and beyond question. Along with Croft and Agnes and Oliver, he had been with the group from the beginning. He was not the most powerful figure in the organization, but he was the most feared.

There were no pleasantries exchanged, his work was pleasure enough for him. "You have an assignment for me, Agnes?"

"Jake Ingram is in Portland," Agnes said. "Do whatever you need in order to stop him from reaching Redemption."

His flat gaze slid to her breasts. His relationship to Agnes was an issue about which even her husband didn't dare speculate. "He travels with bodyguards," he said. "The security around him is too tight for a clean strike."

"That's immaterial. It's vital that he doesn't reach here before Gideon's work is complete."

Prego moved to stand beside her. He ran his tongue over his lips. "And then?"

"And then you may kill Gideon as well."

Gideon felt the burn in his triceps. He clenched his jaw and curled the bar toward his shoulders anyway. The extra weight he'd added to each end was just what he needed. It made him concentrate, made him focus. For as long as his workout lasted, he could shut out everything but the need to push his muscles into giving him one more repetition. Simple. Mindless. As physically satisfying as swinging a crowbar at a locked door.

He lowered the weight slowly, watching his reflection in the mirrored wall to ensure he maintained his alignment. The exercise room had every device necessary to keep a body in optimum physical shape. Gideon's quarters had no room for him to run, so there was a treadmill. He had no access to sunshine, so the tanning bed beside the weight bench provided an artificial source of vitamin D. The whirlpool tub would soak away any stiffness, the cleverly positioned jets pulsing like a masseur's fingers.

Yes, he was well provided for here. He should be content.

He gritted his teeth and forced one more repetition from muscles that he'd pushed beyond their limits. He'd need at least twenty minutes in the whirlpool to unkink the knots he'd formed. He didn't care. The pain was better than his thoughts.

Had Agnes lied to him yesterday? He wanted to believe she had, but the memory she had stirred bore out her words. Reason dictated that he give up his search and get on with the task he'd promised to do. After all, his mind was his greatest asset, right? It was why he had been created in the first place. It was why he had the flaw that could kill him. The Coalition was keeping him alive. Agnes and Oliver were searching for a solution to his fatal flaw. He shouldn't defy them. He should give up this pointless quest into his past. He already didn't like what he'd found.

He released the bar and let the weight drop. It struck the carpet with a thud, bounced twice and came to rest at the foot of the bench. Despite the exhaustion that trembled through his muscles, Gideon was filled with restlessness. He paced the confines of the room, his fists clenched at his side as he tried to keep the troubling thoughts at bay.

But it was no use. Something didn't ring true. What

about the memory of the carefree children playing on the beach? Laughter. Pride. Belonging. How could the warmth he remembered fit if his life had been as bleak as Agnes had described?

And what about the way he felt around Brooke? How could he have recognized her kindness if he'd never experienced it before?

Maybe it was only wishful thinking, a desperate attempt by a freak of science to find something human in his soul. The belated development of a conscience. Why else had he been content to exist like this for all these years?

Or had he been content? It wasn't only his early childhood that was a blank. Many memories of his life here were hazy. Why was that? Was he doing what Brooke had said, blocking out the bad memories? Had he deliberately forgotten the extent of the evil he had done?

He returned to the weight bench. He added an extra five pounds to the bar. A double set of reps had him breathing hard but no closer to relief. He hadn't expected any. The source of his restlessness wasn't physical.

"Excuse me, Gideon."

It was Oliver's voice, sounding oddly apologetic. Gideon put down the barbell and leaned over, bracing his hands on his knees to catch his breath. "What now?"

"I have good news. We have located the Van Gogh and have sent three of our best people to acquire it. The Renoir you requested has been decontaminated and is in the airlock with your evening meal."

It had begun, then, he thought. They had kept their half of the bargain. They would expect him to keep his. "Fine."

"How is your work progressing?"

He lifted his head, looking through the damp strands of hair that had pulled loose to hang in front of his face. He fixed his gaze on the place where the camera was installed behind the mirror. "Fine."

"I'm pleased to hear that. Our contact in the FBI says that Ingram is still in Portland."

Gideon said nothing. He had a grudging respect for the man who had pursued him through cyberspace for the past several months. No one else had come this close to tracking him down before. Jake Ingram had proven himself to be a worthy opponent. Croft and the rest were correct to be alarmed.

Gideon should be as well. As Agnes had reminded him, he would likely not survive long enough to stand trial.

"Well, enjoy the gifts, Gideon."

"Gifts?"

"We also obtained the books you wanted."

Books. Oliver must mean the Sherlock Holmes stories. Gideon had asked for them on a whim, but he looked forward to reading them. It would give him something to talk about the next time he saw Brooke.

The next time... He exhaled hard, his mind clearing. Brooke. Yes, there would be a next time. He wasn't ready to admit defeat. There *were* good memories mixed with the bad. However strong his urge for self-preservation might be, he wasn't ready to give up his search for the truth. Not yet. If it led to his death, then so be it.

Deep inside he'd known for some time that he couldn't continue to live like this.

He straightened up, feeling his muscles flex as he uncoiled to his full height. "I intend to enjoy everything, Oliver."

"Good, good."

"One more thing."

"Yes?"

"Don't disturb me again until tomorrow."

"If there's an emergency—"

"I need a full night's sleep if I'm to complete the programming for the next robbery. My mind will not perform at its optimum without sufficient rest."

"Yes, you've told us that already but—"

"This is nonnegotiable. If I am interrupted during my scheduled rest period again, our deal is off." He turned his back on the mirror and walked to the shower room. He felt a twinge of unease over his insistence—it wasn't wise to let the Coalition know that anything was important or they could use it as a bargaining chip—but he couldn't risk having his nightly trips away from the compound exposed.

Especially now. With Ingram closing in, if Gideon didn't discover the truth about himself soon, he might never get the chance again.

"Is the radio broke? What the hell is that shit?"

Brooke gritted her teeth and strove for patience. The three men who had come in forty minutes ago had finished their burgers and would be leaving soon. God, she hoped they would be leaving soon. She'd thought the place would have been empty by now. She picked up the CD case from the counter and read the title of the track that was playing. "It's Albinoni's 'Adagio in G Minor.'"

"Wrong. It ain't minor. It's major shit." The loudest one of the group laughed at his own joke and jabbed the short man beside him in the ribs. "Get it? *Major* shit?"

"Geez, Rudy, take it easy. That hurts."

The loud man jabbed him again. "You don't know what pain is, Jeff. Back when I was still logging and that fir rolled on my foot—"

"You already told us that story five times." The third man at the table pushed to his feet. "I need a beer if I'm going to hear it again. Let's go to the Wheel."

Brooke hoped his friends would take his suggestion. He was referring to the Wagonwheel Tavern, one of the bars in Redemption that was popular with the blue-collar crowd. Still, if the smell of alcohol she'd noticed when she'd served them was anything to go by, these three had already visited at least one bar before they'd shown up here.

The loud one they had called Rudy tilted his head and smiled at her. He was a large, fleshy man. The unshaved beard stubble on his face bristled in uneven patches as it stretched over his thick jaw. "Come on, honey. Be a sport. You can give us a drink, can't you?"

"I've told you, sir," Brooke said. "We don't serve liquor here."

He stood, hooking his thumbs into his belt as he swaggered toward the counter. "You've got a bottle around somewhere, don't you? We could have a party. Celebrate New Year's Eve a few days early, what do you say?"

Brooke now regretted not asking these men to leave when they'd first started to get obnoxious, but she'd felt sorry for them. Judging from their conversation, which had been loud enough to be impossible not to overhear, they had been laid off from the pulp mill last spring, just some of the many victims of the recent economic downturn.

Lord knew, she had sympathy for people who suffered due to circumstances beyond their control. She was no stranger to rowdy customers, either—when the mill had still been running at full capacity, paydays had brought plenty of lumberjacks who had drunk most of their bonus. Unfortunately, this particular man was crossing the line from annoying to ugly. She picked up her order pad, ripped off the top sheet and placed it on the counter. "Here's your bill, sir."

"Well, that's not very friendly, is it?"

"I'd like you to pay it and leave now, please."

"What I'd *like* is for you to take off that apron and come out from behind that counter." He hitched one hip onto a stool and patted his knee. "Come sit on ol' Rudy's lap."

She shifted her gaze to his companions who were still hovering near their table. Rather than egging him on, they appeared embarrassed by ol' Rudy's behavior. "Would you like me to call a taxi for you?" she asked. "Or would you like me to call Sheriff Woodall? He often stops by here just before closing time. If I ask him, I'm sure he'd give you a ride in the back of the cruiser.''

For a moment no one moved. The quiet strains of the Albinoni adagio swayed in the air, providing a refined contrast to the coarse scene. Brooke lifted her hand toward the phone that hung on the wall behind her to show she was prepared to back up her bluff.

Evidently, they understood her warning. ''Aw, hell. Don't call Woodall.'' The short man named Jeff dug his wallet from his pocket and walked to the counter. He laid out just enough money to cover their bill, then zipped his parka closed and headed for the door. ''This one's on me, Rudy. We don't need that kind of trouble. Let's go to the Wheel like Hank said.''

Brooke let her arm drop and returned her gaze to the leader of the group. ''They have better music,'' she said, offering him a way to leave without losing face.

''Yeah.'' Rudy got off the stool slowly. ''Yeah, they don't play this fairy shit.'' He watched her as he rubbed his hand over his crotch. ''And here I was all set to give you a tip you'd never forget.''

Brooke ignored his lewd gesture and stayed by the phone until the men had left the restaurant. She waited until she saw the red taillights of their truck move out of the parking lot to the highway, then heaved a sigh and went to clear their table.

Mabel was standing in the doorway to the kitchen when Brooke returned with the dishes. ''Why didn't you call for help?'' she asked.

Brooke turned sideways to move past her. ''I don't

like getting involved with the police, but I would have called if it had gotten worse.''

"That Rudy character is a pig," Mabel said, pivoting to keep her in sight.

"Being a pig isn't illegal, or the jails would be overflowing." Brooke dumped the dishes into the sink. "Until Rudy got crude, I felt sorry for them. Those guys have been out of work for months. Tough times can bring out the worst in people.''

"Only if the worst is already there to begin with. Quit making excuses for them. Some people are just plain bad.''

"Or they're forced to become that way.''

Mabel rolled her eyes and turned away. "You're too softhearted, Brooke. You'd find excuses for the devil himself. I'm going to go lock up.''

"Lock up? Already?" Brooke left the dishes and followed her out of the kitchen. "It isn't even eleven-thirty.''

"It's been slow all evening." Mabel crossed the room to the front door and shot the dead bolt. "The week between Christmas and New Year's is always dead. Besides, I've got an appointment with a banker in Portland tomorrow morning and want to get an early start.''

"I can keep the place open on my own," Brooke said.

Mabel flipped the sign on the door. "I would have thought you'd be happy to pack it in considering your last customers.''

"No, really. I don't mind. Please, I'll lock up later.''

"Why don't you want to leave? Are you expecting

someone?'' Mabel paused. Her gaze sharpened. ''That's it, isn't it? I should have realized.''

''What?''

''That's why you put on that dress.'' She walked around her, giving her a slow perusal. ''I like the color. That midnight blue makes your eyes sparkle. Or maybe the sparkle is from something else?''

''Mabel—''

''No wonder you told those jerks the sheriff was going to stop in before closing time. You knew all along Trevor was on his way.''

''Mabel, I'm not expecting Trevor and I didn't dress up for him. He told me he's going to be busy with that FBI business for the rest of the week.'' Brooke brushed some crumbs from her sleeve, realizing this slim-fitting velour wasn't the most practical wardrobe choice. ''And I know you mean well, but why are you pushing him at me all the time?''

''Am I?''

''Yes. And I wish you'd stop.''

''Sorry you feel I'm pushing.'' Mabel held up her palms and stepped back. She didn't sound the least bit contrite. ''What have you got against him, anyway? He might not be all that polished, but he's a good man at heart. He reminds me a little of my second husband. Ian was like one of those big Labrador retrievers that knocks over the furniture because they're so eager to say hello. Come to think of it, that sheepskin coat Trevor likes to wear is the exact color of a yellow Lab.''

''You divorced Ian,'' Brooke pointed out.

Mabel grimaced. ''So I did.''

"Why?"

She glanced at the door, then returned her gaze to Brooke and winked. "He didn't ring my bell."

"Well, Trevor doesn't ring mine."

"No chimes?"

"Not even a jingle."

"Too bad." Mabel tilted her head. "Then why did you dress up, Brooke?"

She should have known Mabel wouldn't let it drop. Brooke took a cloth from her apron pocket and wiped the top of the nearest table. "Lately I haven't had much time to get out. It's the holiday season. I felt like being a bit festive, that's all."

"And what's with the classical music?"

Brooke rubbed harder. "The CD was on sale. I thought I'd try something different."

Mabel caught her elbow and turned her around. "At the risk of ruining my image by getting mushy here, I'm concerned about you, Brooke. I wasn't kidding when I said you were working too hard. The way you do all that baking every morning and then help me the rest of the day is going to wear you out."

"I waitress because you're my friend and you need my help," she said. "I'll never forget how you were there for me when I needed you. I bake because I want to get my business off the ground by next year. You know how important that is to me."

"Yes, I know. I understand. It was the same with me when I opened this restaurant, and I wish you all the success in the world. You deserve it."

"I hear a *but* in your voice."

"But don't do what I did."

"What?"

"Maybe it's the holiday season, or maybe, God forbid, I'm getting sentimental in my old age, but I see a lot of myself in you." Mabel released Brooke's arm and waved her hand to encompass the empty room. "After my third divorce, I was determined to make it on my own. I put everything I had into this business because I thought it would make me happy. The real reason was because I hoped if I kept busy enough, I wouldn't have the chance to get hurt by another man."

"Mabel—"

"I know you have good reason to be cautious, Brooke. What you went through with Frank takes a long time to heal. That's the main reason you didn't call for help tonight, isn't it? You wanted to prove you could face trouble down without running."

Brooke realized there was a lot of truth in what Mabel said. Each time she handled bullies like Rudy without flinching, she threw another shovel full of dirt on the past she'd buried.

"Just don't get so good at dealing with the pigs that you forget there are a few nice ones out there," Mabel said. "You've got such a warm heart, I don't want to see you end up alone."

But I'm not alone, Brooke thought. *I'm waiting for Gideon.*

Or was that just another way of avoiding the chance of getting hurt?

She mulled over what Mabel had said as she dimmed the lights and returned to the kitchen with her to finish cleaning up and prepare for the next day. Mabel's insights shouldn't surprise her, because only a real friend would know her that well, and would feel entitled to speak her mind.

Brooke had indeed put on her favorite dress because she wanted to look her best for a man. All evening she'd turned around each time the door had opened and had peered through the window to the parking lot, eager for the sight of him. But she wasn't looking for the steady, dependable town sheriff, she was looking for... What? A pirate? A poet?

She didn't know his last name. She didn't know where he was from or where he lived or whether he would come to the grill tonight. Is that why he drew her, because he was mysterious and out of reach? Was he attractive to her because he was inaccessible and thus safe?

Perhaps that was part of it. He was like no other man she'd met before. He was fascinating. Intriguing. He stirred her heart with his innocent loneliness.

He'd been right about classical music. It had intimidated her at first, but once she'd started to listen, she'd been able to hear many different levels to each work. She looked forward to hearing more. It would give them something to talk about the next time she saw him.

But that wouldn't be tonight, she decided twenty minutes later as she turned off the kitchen lights and locked the back door of the restaurant behind her. She walked around to the front after Mabel, waved as Mabel pulled her SUV out of the parking lot, then took out her keys and headed for her car.

At the sound of footsteps behind her, she felt a rush

of anticipation. Had he come after all? She spun around.

A fleshy hand clamped over her arm. "'bout time you got off, honey. Let's go party."

Five

It was a measure of how far she had come from Wichita—and Frank—that Brooke didn't immediately feel fear. No, what she felt first was disgust. She recognized the voice of her assailant as well as the scent of sour beer on his breath. Rudy had returned, and this time there were no witnesses or counter to put between them.

She twisted, trying to pull her arm from his grasp. "Let go of me!"

He tightened his grip and yanked her to the front of his body, bringing his other arm around her back. "I know you want it, honey. I saw the way you were wiggling that ass at me all night. I've got my truck parked over here." He started to drag her toward the shadows at the opposite side of the building. "We'll be real comfortable. It'll be just me and you and a bottle of tequila."

Even through the down padding of her winter coat, she felt his fingers dig into her arm hard enough to bruise. The disgust switched to anger and she jerked her knee upward, aiming for his groin.

Despite his bulk, he moved quickly, taking the brunt of her blow on his thigh. "You bitch," he muttered.

He grabbed a fistful of her hair and yanked back hard. "You want it rough? Okay, we can do that."

The pain in her scalp brought tears to her eyes. It also brought home to her the seriousness of her situation. Even if she broke free of him, where could she go? He would probably be able to catch up with her before she could unlock the door of the grill. Same with her car. The highway was empty, and even if a vehicle happened to go past, the driver might not be able to see what was happening.

Oh, God. Why hadn't she called the police earlier? Was it really necessary to prove herself over and over? She screamed, more from the adrenaline that shot through her veins than from any hope that someone might hear. Using her elbows, her feet, her knees, whatever she could move, she fought in earnest to keep him from taking her anywhere.

"Let her go."

The voice was so welcome, she thought she must have imagined it. She twisted her head to look and felt sharp pinpoints of pain as hair ripped from her temple. Through a thickening haze of tears, she saw Gideon appear out of nowhere at the edge of the parking lot.

"Let her go," he repeated, loping forward.

"Get lost," Rudy said. "She's coming with me." He gave Brooke a shake that snapped her teeth shut and kept moving.

Gideon approached at an angle, like a predator circling his prey, until he had positioned himself between them and the pickup that gleamed in the darkness. He spoke in a tone Brooke had never heard him use before. It was as cold as the night around them. "Release her. Now."

"Keep out of this," Rudy said. "It's none of your business."

"Is this your vehicle?" Gideon asked.

Rudy stopped. "Get the hell out of my way."

Gideon moved suddenly, pivoting on one foot to bring his other foot around in an arc toward the truck. The sole of his boot connected with the mirror on the driver's side door. Amid the sound of grating metal and crunching glass, the mirror snapped off to go spinning over the hood.

"Hey!" Rudy yelled. "Hey, get away from that! Are you crazy?"

"Let her go."

"Back off."

Gideon stepped to the side and spun again. The heel of his boot shattered a headlight.

Rudy released his grip on Brooke and thrust her aside so quickly she had to put out her hands to break her fall. She hit the pavement hard and rolled away. In the scant second it took her to come to her knees and look up, Rudy had already reached Gideon and was drawing back his fist.

"Look out!" she cried.

Gideon dodged the first blow, but the second one grazed the side of his head. He staggered backward. He didn't appear hurt, he appeared...surprised.

"You pansy bastard. I'll teach you not to mess with my truck," Rudy said, swinging again. He buried his fist in Gideon's stomach.

Brooke got to her feet, horrified at what appeared

to be an uneven match. Although the men were almost
the same height, Rudy outweighed Gideon by at least
fifty pounds. He also seemed a far more experienced
fighter. He was pressing his advantage, driving Gideon
back against the side of the truck and landing one
vicious punch after another to his belly.

She thought fleetingly of unlocking the restaurant
and calling the police, but from the way the fight was
going, by the time they got here Gideon would need
an ambulance. She was looking around for a weapon,
a rock, a stick, desperate to help him, when Gideon
appeared to figure out how to help himself. He blocked
the next blow with his forearm and smashed his elbow
into Rudy's face.

Blood spurted from Rudy's nose, spattering Gideon's cheek. Rudy screamed and circled Gideon's
neck with his fingers. When Gideon caught his hands
to break his grip, Rudy turned his head and clamped
his teeth on Gideon's wrist where the skin had been
bared below his glove.

Brooke felt her stomach heave at the savage way
Rudy fought. She would have had no chance against
him alone. Yet somehow Gideon shook him off,
hooked his foot behind Rudy's ankles and jerked him
off balance. Before the heavier man reached the
ground, Gideon caught him by the back of his jacket
and his belt and used his momentum to heave him
forward. Rudy thudded headfirst into the fender of the
truck and slid limply to the ground.

Gideon regarded the dent in the fender, then walked
over to where Rudy had landed and nudged him with
his boot to roll him onto his back.

Rudy groaned and clutched his head.

"I advise you to leave while you and your vehicle are still functioning," Gideon said. He leaned over, grasped Rudy by the collar and lifted him to his feet. "Drive away and do not come back."

Rudy's head lolled. Still, he managed a sneer.

Gideon tightened his grip around the larger man's throat.

Rudy's sneer disappeared. He clawed at Gideon's arms.

Gideon held him steady, their gazes locked. "This is not open to negotiation," he said. "If you do not do as I say I will use your body to continue my destruction of your truck, as you do not seem to value either."

"Go to hell."

Gideon pivoted, swinging Rudy in an arc toward the windshield.

Rudy grabbed for Gideon's coat. "Okay, okay!"

Gideon altered direction and released his grip, bouncing Rudy off the door. Another deep dent appeared in the metal. Gideon moved over to stand beside Rudy's head. "Stay away from this place and this woman."

"Crazy bastard," Rudy muttered, scrambling to his knees. He dug in his jacket pocket for his keys and hauled himself into the truck. "The bitch ain't worth this."

Gideon walked purposefully toward the rear taillight. Before he could reach it, Rudy started the engine and screeched out of the parking lot. Gideon waited until the sound of the truck faded down the highway, then turned to look at Brooke.

He was breathing hard. Strands of hair had pulled loose from his queue to float wildly around his face. There was a darkness to his expression that wasn't due to the shadows. Yet when he spoke, his voice wasn't the hard, clipped tone he'd used with Rudy. It was once more as rich and warm as Brooke remembered. "Are you all right?"

Brooke's heart was racing too hard for her to reply. Had she really seen her gentle Gideon turn into a warrior? She swayed, the strength going out of her knees.

He moved forward and reached her before she could fall, catching her by her elbows to steady her. He ducked to look into her face. "Did he hurt you?"

She shook her head. Her scalp stung and her arm throbbed, but she couldn't complain. It could have been so much worse if Gideon hadn't arrived when he had. She laid her palm on the front of his coat. "I'm okay. What about you?"

"I'm sorry I didn't get here sooner."

"I'm lucky you did. He was... Oh, God. I can't believe this happened."

"Brooke?"

She blinked hard against the tears she couldn't control. "I hate this, Gideon. I don't want to be a victim. I don't want to feel powerless, but when he grabbed me—" Her voice broke. She lifted her hand to wipe the blood from his face. "Thank you."

At the touch of her fingers, Gideon tensed. He tipped his face out of her reach.

"You have blood there," she said.

"What?"

"Don't worry, I'm sure it isn't yours. When you hit his nose I saw his blood spray— Oh God, it was horrible."

"I didn't even notice," he said. He wiped his face and stared at the wet smears on the fingertips of his gloves.

She took his hand and turned it over. "What about your wrist?"

"My wrist?"

"I saw him bite you."

Gideon pulled back his sleeve to expose his arm. Beneath the dark hair that sprinkled his wrist, there were twin rows of angry red marks where the top layer of skin was broken. A trace of what had to be saliva still glistened on the wound. He stared at it like a man in a trance. "He bit me."

"He fought like an animal." Now that the danger was over, reaction was setting in fast. Brooke could feel her hands start to shake. She grabbed the edges of Gideon's lapels, digging her fingers into the fine wool to keep herself upright. "We should disinfect your wrist."

He didn't reply.

She hiccuped as she held back a sob. She returned her gaze to his face. "Gideon?"

In silence he stared at her the same way he'd stared at the blood on his gloves and the teeth marks on his skin. A tremor went through his frame.

"Gideon, please," she whispered, raising herself on her toes to bring her face closer to his. "Don't go weird on me now."

He inhaled slowly, his nostrils flaring. A muscle in his jaw twitched as he lifted his hand to her cheek. He paused before he touched her, then slowly, one finger at a time, he pulled off his glove. He held his hand a breath away from her, near enough for her to feel the heat of his skin.

"Gideon?"

Exhaling hard, he closed the gap and caught one of her tears on his bare knuckle.

His expression was like nothing she had seen before. Pain mixed with pleasure. A shadow stirred in the depths of his gaze, an echo of buried rage, yet his lips curved in a smile of such incredible sweetness it went straight to her heart.

She rubbed her cheek against the back of his hand, drying her tears on his skin. "We should probably call the cops."

He tensed again. "The police?"

"But you handled Rudy better than they could. I don't think he'll come back. I just want to go home." She'd been courageous enough for one night, hadn't she? There would be no shame in retreat now. "Please, Gideon, could you take me home?"

Brooke's apartment was small enough to have fitted into one corner of Gideon's library. It was on the top floor of a square, redbrick three-story building. Her front window looked out on a short street lined with other square redbrick three-story buildings. The window over the tub in the bathroom opened to a row of skeletal, half-framed houses on the edge of the forest where expansion of the subdivision had been halted last spring when the worldwide recession hadn't left enough potential buyers to fill the units that had already been constructed.

Those unfinished buildings were because of him, Gideon realized. Another economic repercussion of the World Bank heist. He'd always been adamant that no life would be lost due to his crimes, but there were other more insidious ways in which people could be hurt.

But that was all over. Achilles had stolen his last dime. Never again would he strike one bargain after another to stay alive. There was no longer any need. It should be a relief to have the game finished.

It wasn't. He didn't feel relieved, he felt angry. Cheated. Helpless. He wanted to tip back his head and rage at the unfairness of it.

Yet that would be a waste of time, and time was suddenly limited. Precious. How much living could he pack into what little time he had left?

Gideon let the white lace curtain fall back to block out the darkness, absorbing the way the fabric felt as it slid through his fingers. It looked soft, but it was unexpectedly rough. He moved his hand along the edge of the window, exploring the temperature difference where the wood was close to the glass. There was a blue china saucer on the windowsill that held tiny green spheres. They were soft, gelatinous, with some kind of liquid inside, he discovered when he picked one up. He brought it to his nose. It smelled like fresh snow in the night. Like Brooke.

"Here we go," Brooke said. "You'd better sit down."

He replaced the green sphere and turned to face her. She was unscrewing the top of a small dark-brown glass bottle. Against the pink blush on her cheeks, he saw the pale tracks of dried tears. He lifted his hand and rubbed them off with the pad of his thumb. "It isn't necessary, Brooke."

She swallowed, her gaze going to his lips.

Was he touching her too much? he wondered as he dropped his hand and sat on the edge of the bathtub. He studied her face, trying to guess what she was feeling. He didn't think her blush was from distress. Her trembling had gradually subsided the farther they'd gotten from the grill. He wished he could have driven her car for her, but although he knew how the vehicle worked in principle, he'd never had the opportunity to sit behind a wheel.

But that hadn't mattered to her. She'd asked him to take her home, not because she needed help to get here but because she hadn't wanted to be alone.

Neither did he. And for the first time, there was no longer any need for that, either.

Amid the barrage of new sensations he was discovering, Brooke was the most fascinating by far. Her scent, the curving swell of her hips and her breasts beneath her dress, the fine lines that appeared at the corners of her eyes when she smiled. He could spend years and not fully explore every facet of this woman.

But he didn't have years. The process of his destruction would have already begun. The gamma-aminobutyric acid from the DNA in Rudy's blood and saliva would have passed through Gideon's skin to his veins where it was being pumped to every vulnerable genetically altered cell in his body. His immune system would be gearing up to fight the invader, yet there was no defense as his own altered cells would recognize the missing amino acid and be triggered to replicate it. By tomorrow, Gideon's lungs would begin to fill with fluid. By the next day, his kidneys would start to shut down. His motor control would fail along with his mental functioning. Death wouldn't follow immediately. He could linger for up to a week, but by then he'd no longer be aware of anything except the pain.

"This might hurt," she said, stepping between his knees to take his hand in hers.

She was wrong, Gideon thought as he felt her fingers slide to his wrist to push up the sleeve of his black knit shirt. This was bliss. A human touch. He'd longed for it, wondered about it, read about it. The reality surpassed any dream.

She'd clung to him before they'd left the parking lot. She'd moved into his arms the moment she'd locked the door of this apartment behind them. She'd wanted comfort, and he'd been concerned he wouldn't know how to give it.

No one had asked that of him before. There was no profit in comfort, no power, no bargain. It would have no value in life in the Coalition. It wasn't a skill that came from his genetically enhanced intellect.

Yet it turned out to be amazingly simple. Sympathy, kind words and touch. Always touch. How could he have lived for so many years without it?

He hadn't. He'd merely been existing, not living.

There was a mild sting as the acrid-smelling disinfectant seeped through the broken skin of Rudy's bite, yet it was hardly noticeable. Gideon waited until she was finished, then caught the lock of hair that swung over her shoulder and sifted his fingers through her curls.

Her breasts lifted as she inhaled sharply.

Gideon stilled. "I'm sorry. Your scalp must be sore from where he gripped you."

"No, I'm fine," she said. "Thanks to you."

He'd acted instinctively when he'd heard her scream. He hadn't considered the risk to himself; he'd only wanted to help Brooke. Yet even if he'd taken the time to think, his decision would have been the same. Saving Brooke was the right thing to do.

Not that one good deed could atone for a lifetime of crime, but at least he could die believing the evil inside him wasn't as complete as he'd feared.

He gathered her curls in his palm to cushion his touch as he cupped her head. "You have beautiful hair. It's like the Appalachians in autumn, on fire with the colors of the earth."

"Have you—" She paused and moistened her lips. "Have you been there?"

"Only through books." He leaned forward to bring her hair to his nose. "Your scent intrigues me, Brooke. You're a feast for the senses. How do you use the spheres of liquid that are in the saucer?"

"The spheres…" She paused. "You mean the bath oil beads?"

"Ah. Now I understand." He rubbed her hair against his lips, then released it and smiled. "The gelatin would dissolve in the warm water of your bath."

"That's right."

He skimmed his palm over her sleeve, tilting his head to study the play of light on the soft velour. "And when you immerse yourself in the tub your naked skin would absorb the oil."

She fumbled behind her to set the bottle of disinfectant on the sink. "I'd better put a bandage on your wrist."

"Why?"

"You don't want that iodine to stain your sweater."

"I'll roll up the sleeve," he said, folding the thin knit fabric above his elbow.

The color in her cheeks deepened as her gaze moved over his bare forearm. "No wonder you were able to toss Rudy around the way you did," she murmured. "You're..." She cleared her throat. "Very strong."

"I was unsure how to overpower him at first. I'm unaccustomed to using physical force as a negotiating tool."

"Well, you're a fast learner." She traced a ridge of muscle up his arm with her fingertip. "The way you went after his truck was smart. It worked really well."

His arm tensed beneath her light caress. "I've learned the best way to have people do what you want is to bargain with something they value."

"I wish I could have helped you. I felt sick when I saw how he was punching your stomach."

"After the first blow I flexed my abdominals so that he wouldn't injure me." He pulled up his sweater and curled forward to check the damage. The skin over his solar plexus was reddened and beginning to purple.

"Oh, my God!" Brooke dropped to her knees in

front of the tub and put her hand on his stomach. "Gideon, I'm sorry. I should have realized you were hurt."

Until now he'd ignored the throbbing ache from these bruises. He'd had too many other more pleasant sensations to absorb. "It looks worse than it feels."

Her fingers fluttered over his ribs. "You got these bruises because of me."

"It was worth it, Brooke."

"It must have hurt like hell."

"I didn't notice at the time."

"Maybe you should get X-rayed. What if you have a broken rib? It should be wrapped or something."

"No, I believe my ribs are all intact." He placed his palm over her hand and held it still. The lower edge of his sweater fell over his wrist, enclosing their hands beneath. "I don't need a bandage, either. Your touch is all I need. It's like the slide of silk in the darkness. It makes my skin come alive with sparks of sensation."

Her lips parted. She looked at him in silence, her eyes luminous. He could feel the puff of her breath with each rapid rise and fall of her chest.

Understanding finally dawned. Gideon recognized what Brooke was feeling, because he was feeling it himself. It had been building since they had arrived at Brooke's apartment. His own breathing was growing faster. His pulse was beating heavily. His blood was pumping to his groin so hard his mind was shutting down.

He was no stranger to the sensation. There was enough of the human male in him to have a full complement of normal male sexual urges. He wasn't ignorant about the topic, either—his library contained volumes of information about sex, everything from the *Kama Sutra* to the *Kinsey Report*—yet Gideon had always believed that his knowledge would have to remain theoretical.

When he'd been younger, he'd tried to find an outlet for his needs through erotic fantasies and self-gratification, but that temporary relief fell far short of the satisfaction he craved. So he'd tried to suppress his urges and channel his energy into exercise or into the intellectual demands of his work on the security devices for Redcom.

But the sexual urges that had plagued him over the years couldn't compare to the need he felt now. He didn't simply want physical gratification, he wanted Brooke.

He looked at her mouth, so close to his. How would her lips feel if he stroked them with his tongue? He rotated his hand until he could slide his fingers between hers and wondered how it would feel to join their bodies. He wanted to touch her, taste her, explore her scent and her texture, watch her respond to all the intimacies he'd studied and dreamed of yet had never experienced.

And he could think of no better way to spend the time he had left.

Six

This was happening too fast, Brooke thought, feeling her blood throb heavily in every pulse point in her body. They were in her bathroom, for pity's sake. This was only the third time she'd seen Gideon. In so many ways he was still a stranger, yet here she was, kneeling between his thighs, her hand pressed to his bare chest and her mouth so ready for his kiss, her lips were aching.

Why? Was it a reaction to the violence of an hour ago? A result of her fear and her gratitude?

No, it was a reaction to Gideon. What normal woman wouldn't react like this? The way he spoke was so sensual, each word was a caress. He was looking at her with a poignant mixture of desire and regret, like a condemned man regarding his last meal. The hunger in his gaze made her feel more than wanted, she felt...necessary. It was a heady feeling, to be needed that intensely.

And then there was his body. What normal woman could ignore a physique like Gideon's? She lowered her gaze to the place where his sweater folded over their joined hands. She'd suspected he was in good shape because of the way he moved, but she hadn't guessed how good. From what she could see—and feel—he was all muscle and sinew, a perfectly toned male. She flexed her hand, fitting her palm to the washboard ripples on his abdomen.

She could feel the heat of a bruise. Was there something wrong with her that she found it…exciting? He had fought for her and rescued her. He'd come home with her and comforted her. The night that had started out so ugly was turning into something…

What? Magical? She didn't believe in magic. Or fate or romance. No love-at-first-sight fairy tales for her, no, not any more. She was a realist. Her dreams didn't depend on a man to come true. As Mabel would say, there were far more Franks and Rudys in the world than good ones like Gideon.

Was Gideon one of the good ones? Judging by his actions tonight, he definitely was. She'd never known a man could be so tough and physical one minute and then so sensitive the next. If someone did believe in fairy tales, Gideon would be well suited to play the role of the gallant knight.

She sighed in pleasure as he brought their joined hands to his mouth. He dragged her fingers across his lower lip, touching each with the tip of his tongue, then tilted his head and plunged his tongue through the V at the base of her fingers.

Reaction shuddered through her body. She had never felt anything so gently erotic. It was as if he were making love to her hand. She swayed against his thigh.

He caught her thumb between his teeth, his eyelids half closed. A sound that could have been a question or could have been pleasure rumbled from his chest. "Brooke?"

Her senses were so immersed in what he was doing, it was difficult for her to form words. "Mmm?"

"Do you want me to stop?"

"I should. I haven't done…this for years."

"You mean sex?"

His bluntness jarred her, yet how else would Gideon approach the subject? "Yes, I mean sex."

"I want to make love to you, Brooke. Tonight. Now."

Her body replied to his bold declaration with a surge of liquid need. "Gideon…"

"Would you like that?"

She marveled that he was waiting for an answer. Considering the signals she must have been putting out since they got to her apartment, it had to be obvious. "Oh, yes, Gideon."

He smiled, spread her fingers wide and pressed his mouth to her palm.

Brooke felt an answering quiver between her thighs.

"It's not the same," he murmured. "I need you to know that."

"What?"

He slipped his hands under her arms and stood, lifting her to her feet. "What I want and what Rudy wanted."

Again, she wondered if there was something wrong with her. The reminder of Rudy's attempted assault should have doused the pleasure that was building. It didn't. Instead it made Gideon's touch all the more welcome. This was what she needed to drive the bad memory away. She put her hands on his shoulders, exploring their breadth, enjoying the tautness. He was a powerful man, but he held his power in check. He wouldn't hurt her. "I know it's different. Because you're different. You're not like any man I've met before."

He looked at her, his smile fading. "And I have never in my life known anyone like you, Brooke. Your warmth draws me. Your compassion humbles me. There are so many aspects of you I want to know, but this urge I feel is so strong…" He clenched his jaw.

She caught his face. "Gideon?"

At the touch of her palms on his cheeks, his chest heaved. "I want to feel your skin on mine," he said. His voice was rough, his words raw and hurried, as if he feared he wouldn't have enough time to say them all. "I want to feel your hair loose and flowing between my fingers, your legs wrapped around my hips, your nails scoring my back, your scent in my lungs and your taste in my mouth…" He trailed off. He cupped her breast, his hand shaking. "I want you so much, Brooke, I don't know where to start."

His tenderness had already touched her heart just as his need had already seduced her body. The vulnerability he was letting her see now drove away the last of Brooke's caution. What did it matter where they were or how long she'd known him? Nothing in her life before had felt so right. She covered his hand, holding it against her breast. "You already started a week ago, Gideon, when you let me see your loneliness."

His hand steadied. Squeezed. Kneaded. With his

other hand he grasped the back of her neck. Slowly, oh, far too slowly, he lowered his head.

Brooke stretched up and closed the gap herself, sealing her mouth to his.

He shuddered.

She parted her lips.

For a moment he didn't respond to her invitation. Then as naturally as drawing breath, he slid his tongue inside. His mouth moved over hers as if he wanted to explore every nuance of sensation. He nibbled. He tasted. He kissed her with such thoroughness that Brooke hadn't realized he had eased her dress off her shoulders until she felt his thumb slide beneath the edge of her bra to circle her nipple.

She moaned at the contact. When Gideon started to withdraw his hand, she pressed closer. "Don't stop," she whispered. "That feels so good."

This time there was no hesitation. He unhooked her bra, tossed it aside and bent to press his lips to her breast. He kissed her with the same thoroughness he'd used on her mouth, teasing her with his lips and his tongue and his teeth until Brooke had no strength left in her legs to stand.

He caught her by the waist and yanked off the rest of her clothes. She heard something rip but she didn't care. She was trembling now, her senses whirling and so tight she was on the verge of shattering. He swung her into his arms and carried her to her bedroom. He wasted no time laying her on the mattress and stripping off his own clothes, yet he wasn't ready to finish. Despite her whispered pleas to urge him on faster, he stretched out beside her and resumed his exploration of her body.

The first climax hit without warning. She wasn't even sure what he'd done to trigger it. The brush of his hair on her navel? The heat of his breath on her thigh? His fingers? His thumb? She fisted her hands in the sheet. "Gideon!"

He licked the back of her knee and slid his hand between her legs.

The next climax sent her arching off the bed. She fought to draw air into her lungs, too astonished to make a sound. Before the tremors had ended, he draped her leg over his shoulder, curled forward and gave her a third.

Brooke wasn't sure if she screamed, the rush of her pulse in her ears was too loud. She inhaled on a sob. This was too much. Too much. Yet not nearly enough. She wriggled out of his hold and reached for him. "Gideon, please."

She gasped as he filled her. He was shaking again. She could feel the power of his need with every shift of his hips. She was ready, so ready, but he moved as if each moment were precious, as if he wanted to savor the age-old rhythm of ebb and flow, the sounds of their bodies meeting, the scents of sweat and sex.

Yet it was more than sex, she realized as she focused on his face. It was a joining of two people, the ultimate form of human contact. His gaze was as naked as his body, and the lost-child longing she saw there was so strong it brought tears to her eyes.

She wasn't sure she understood it. She decided she

didn't need to. She wrapped herself around him and held on as if she'd never have to let him go.

Gideon felt as if a layer of dulling film had been ripped from his senses. Everything was so vivid. The colors on the flowered sheets that covered the bed, the sound of the hot water flowing through the radiator under the window. The feel of Brooke's slender fingers as she played with the hair on his chest. The satisfaction that sang through his lax muscles. And the anger that burned in his soul.

How could he have discovered this only to lose it? Damn, *damn*, this hadn't been a wise idea. Wouldn't he have been better off not knowing what he'd missed all these years?

The thought hadn't fully formed before he was rejecting it. No. He had no regrets about what he and Brooke had done. How could he? It would have been far worse to die without knowing what he'd missed.

But he didn't want to die. Not yet. Not when he felt so alive in every nerve in his body. Not when he finally had more than simply himself to live for.

"Are you drifting off again?"

At Brooke's question, he drove the anger back to the dark corner where it dwelled. He smiled and caught her hand. "What do you mean?"

"Sometimes you get this faraway look in your eyes and it's like you're not here."

"There's nowhere I'd rather be than here in this bed with you," he said, pressing his nose to her knuckles. He inhaled deeply, drawing in the scent of her skin mixed with the scent of his own. "I apologize if I seemed inattentive."

She made a choking sound, then rolled toward him, burying her face against his chest. Her shoulders shook.

He stroked her back, concerned. "Brooke? Is something wrong?"

She lifted her head. The golden glow of the bedside lamp revealed the edges of her lips were trembling. "Gideon, if you'd been any more attentive, you would have killed me."

"You're joking," he murmured. "Right?"

She laughed and stretched to kiss his chin. "Yes, I'm kidding."

None of the books he'd read mentioned that humor could be mixed with sex, but it felt like a natural extension of the intimacy. Gideon settled her more comfortably on top of him and hooked one leg over hers. "I don't believe the words have been written that could describe how you make me feel, Brooke. It's as if all the goodness in the world was distilled to its essence and hidden in your smile."

Sighing, she folded her arms on his chest so that she didn't lean on his bruises and rested her chin on her hand. "Are you sure you work at Taber Aviation?"

"What do you mean?"

"You could make a nice living as a poet."

"Believe me, there's no demand for anything as frivolous as poetry where I work."

"It's not frivolous, it's…oh, I don't know how to put it. Like taking ordinary language and turning it into something unexpected and beautiful. Like music.''

''Ah. Food for the soul.''

''Exactly.'' She picked up a lock of his hair and twirled it around her finger. ''I bought a CD of a collection of classical music at the mall the other day. I had to listen to it a few times but I discovered I like it. Especially Chopin. The CD has one of his waltzes on it.''

''It's not surprising that you'd like his work. It has a certain tenderness to it that reminds me of you.''

She stroked the ends of his hair along his jaw. ''I'm glad you gave me the idea to try it.''

''And I must thank you for telling me about Doyle. I particularly enjoyed 'The Speckled Band.'''

''Which one was that?''

''That was the story about the man who was locked in a supposedly impregnable room, but there was a way in and out after all. Sherlock Holmes is an ingenious character.''

''Very logical.''

He smiled. ''Yes.''

''I like your hair. It looks downright scandalous when it's loose like this.''

He turned his head to kiss her hand. He'd never concerned himself with his appearance and he didn't have access to a barber, so he'd never thought much about his hair. Tying it at the nape of his neck was practical. When his hair got too long, he simply gathered it in his fist and lopped it off with shears. ''I like what you're doing with it.''

''Ever thought of wearing an earring?'' She touched

his earlobe. "Maybe a gold stud or a kind of pirate hoop?"

He noticed the humor at the corners of her eyes and realized she was joking again. He sat up, propped a pair of pillows behind his back and drew her onto his lap. "Only if it means you don't want me to wear anything else."

She laughed and stroked his arm, curling her fingers around his biceps. "You drive a hard bargain, but I suppose a girl could get used to seeing you like this." She hesitated. "Do you mind if I ask you something, Gideon? It's kind of a weird question, considering."

"Go ahead."

"What's your last name?"

That threw him. Until tonight, he'd been careful not to give her any information about himself, yet what did it matter now? As long as he didn't give her any knowledge that might put her in danger from the law or the Coalition, what was stopping him from confiding in her?

He'd never confided in anyone. He'd been as alone with his thoughts as he had been with his body. This would be another new sensation, another level of intimacy to experience.

It was surprising how much he wanted it. He pulled her closer, wrapping his arms around her back. "As far as I know, it's Faulkner."

"What do you mean?"

"I was…adopted as a child. That's the name I was given."

"Oh." She studied his face, her eyebrows lifting.

"Oh! Now I understand. That's why you couldn't tell me about your childhood."

"Yes. I remember very little about my early years. My life before I was ten is essentially a blank."

"Ten years? That's so sad." She stroked his jaw. "The other night in the restaurant when you were talking about the children on the beach, was that one of those memories?"

"Yes, I believe the children might have been my siblings."

"I can understand now why you looked so shaken up. It must have been horrible to be separated from them. No wonder you blocked it out."

Was that true? Could the emotional trauma of losing his family have contributed to his memory loss?

His family? Or the other test subjects who had been shot by the woman who had loaned her womb to Code Proteus? Which interpretation was right?

"What about your adoptive parents? Do they know your background?"

"It's a...touchy subject. The people who raised me would prefer me to forget it. I'm not sure if I can believe what they've told me but I haven't wished to confront them."

Brooke's gaze was filled with a quiet sympathy. "Have you thought about looking for your real family? I've heard there's a national registry where people who have been adopted can link up with their birth parents."

"I doubt if they would be on it," he replied. "I had been using other avenues to search for information about my past."

"You sound as if you aren't looking anymore."

"It no longer seems relevant." He felt a twinge of renewed anger over the lost opportunity to discover the truth. He tamped it down. He didn't want to waste his time with anger. He was dying. Any further truth about himself was irrelevant. "What about you, Brooke? Do you have any siblings?"

"No. It was just my mother and me when I was growing up."

"In the apartment above the bakery that smelled like fresh bread."

"Pretty corny, I know."

"No, Brooke, it sounds wonderful. And now it's your turn."

"Mmm?"

"What's your last name?"

"Carter."

Had she hesitated before she'd replied? Had he made a mistake by asking like this? He might understand the mechanics of sex, but he knew nothing about relationships. He gave her a light kiss. "Pleased to meet you, Brooke Carter."

"Likewise, Gideon Faulkner." She snuggled closer. "You were right, by the way. I probably do want to start up my own bakery so I can recapture some of the good times."

"I hope you succeed."

"Thanks. As long as the bank I'm counting on this time doesn't collapse, I might have a chance."

"Do you need financing?"

"Me, Mabel and everyone else in the country after Achilles cleaned us all out."

He dropped his forehead against hers, not wanting her to see the wave of guilt that went through him. He thought about the unfinished buildings at the end of the street and the innumerable banks that had collapsed. How many more broken dreams was he responsible for? "I'm sorry, Brooke."

"Why? It's not as if you took that money."

"It isn't fair that innocent people like you suffered. You did nothing."

"None of us is totally innocent," she murmured. "I think, given the right circumstances..."

When she didn't continue, he put his hand under her chin to tip her face toward his. "Brooke?"

She shook her head. "Let's change the subject, okay? Life's too short for regrets."

He rubbed his cheek against hers, focusing on her warmth, her kindness, her goodness. "I couldn't agree with you more."

"That's why I'm not going to regret tonight," she said firmly.

"I'm glad, Brooke. Being here with you is unlike anything I've known before. I wish..."

"What do you wish, Gideon?"

Her question brought a flash of pain. He wished the night would never end.

He wished they could stay like this forever.

He wished he was human.

"I wish that I'd found you sooner," he said finally.

She was silent for a while before she pulled back to look at him again. "Do you want to try something really decadent?"

He'd thought his body was sated. Furthermore, he'd

thought his guilt would have snuffed out any desire that was left. But at her whispered suggestion, his mind instantly filled with images from some of the less widely circulated books that he'd read. His blood surged. He rubbed his foot over her calf and shifted his hips. "Whatever you'd like, Brooke. I've been told I'm a fast learner."

She laughed and slid off him. "Stay there," she said, drawing on a faded green terry cloth robe. "I'll be right back."

He gave her thirty seconds before he got up and followed her. He found her in the alcove in the corner of the living room that served as her kitchen. She was leaning over the open door of a small white refrigerator, silhouetted by the dim glow of light that came from within. Her robe covered her from her neck to her ankles, yet the mere thought of what that robe concealed made Gideon groan.

She straightened up and looked over her shoulder. Her eyes widened. "Forget the earring," she murmured. "It would be a crime to add even that much."

There was no humor in her expression as she gazed at his naked body, only what he now recognized as desire. He moved forward.

She swallowed. "I was going to come back to bed."

"I'd prefer not to wait," he said, stopping behind her. He slid his hands around her waist, then splayed them over the front of her thighs and drew her against him.

She let the refrigerator door swing shut, leaving them in darkness. Her head fell back on his shoulder. "Open your mouth, Gideon."

He felt the brush of her fingers on his lips and he did as she asked. Something soft touched his tongue. Seconds later, a symphony of flavor exploded through his senses.

She laughed softly. "It's a chocolate and rum eggnog eclair. I told you it was decadent."

He had a moment of automatic, gut-level panic. He couldn't eat this. It hadn't been treated. He couldn't risk—

He almost laughed. He could risk anything because he had nothing left to lose. He closed his eyes and chewed. The pastry dissolved into a swirl of buttery flakes. The top note of chocolate gave way to a deeper undertone of mingled tastes too fleeting to name.

It was as different from the bland, specially prepared food that kept him alive as real sex was from the illustrations in his books. He was grateful now that he hadn't eaten any of the dinner that had been left for him tonight; he'd been too eager to leave the compound to care about nourishment. He nuzzled Brooke's fingers, feeling suddenly greedy. "More."

She fed him another bite. "What do you think?"

He moved his hands to the front of her robe, parted the edges and swept the fabric aside. "I think I'm starving, Brooke."

Seven

The slam of the restaurant's back door brought Brooke awake with a start. Her foot slipped off the rung of the stool. Blinking, she lifted her head from her folded arms. She'd intended to sit down at the work table for only a moment.

Mabel shook the snow off her coat and hung it up on the rack beside the door. "Damn bankers," she muttered. "They're as bad as politicians."

Brooke swallowed a yawn as she straightened up. "Mabel, what are you doing here? I thought you had an appointment at a bank in Portland."

"The little weasel cancelled. I found his message on my machine when I got home last night. He said seeing as they were predicting snow in this area he wanted to save me the trip since he wasn't going to give me the loan at the rate I wanted anyway. Bankers are a bunch of loan-sharking crooks, if you ask me."

"Oh, Mabel. I'm so sorry. Is there anything I can do?"

"You're already doing too much." Mabel tucked her newspaper under her arm and snagged a second stool as she crossed the kitchen. "You were asleep when I got here, weren't you?"

"I might have dozed off for a minute."

Brooke glanced at the clock. "Or five. Don't worry about me."

"Well, don't worry about me, either. I've got a lead on a widower in Salem who's looking to invest in something safer than a bank, so I'm not too broken up about the banker. The weasel." Mabel positioned the stool in her usual spot under the light and put on her reading glasses. "By the way, whatever you're making smells downright decadent."

Brooke smiled, recalling Gideon's unrestrained enjoyment when she'd fed him a sample of her baking the night before. "Uh-huh, it is. Chocolate and rum eggnog eclairs." She rolled her head to work out some stiffness in her neck. "The filling is in that bowl by the sink. Go ahead and try some if you want."

Mabel detoured to the sink and dipped a spoon into the bowl. "You've outdone yourself, Brooke. This is…" She frowned, lifting her head to sniff. "Uh-oh. Is something burning?"

Brooke grabbed a pair of protective mitts and raced for the oven.

The last batch of puff pastry wasn't the delicate gold of the other shells that lined the cooling rack. The color was closer to burnt leather. Brooke sighed and dumped the lot in the garbage.

She should probably be upset—this was a special order for a holiday open house at the residence of Redemption's mayor, and the exposure could lead to a jump in her business—but she was feeling too mellow to be upset. The batch was spoiled because she'd fallen asleep. She'd fallen asleep because Gideon had made love to her most of the night. How could she be anything but mellow?

She'd never been a big fan of sex—it was pleasant but overrated as far as she'd been concerned. Yet what Gideon had done had been totally…intoxicating. Where on earth had he learned to use his body that way? He'd been so sweet and yet so incredibly sexy, she got tingles whenever she remembered what they'd done together.

Intoxicating and habit-forming. She could hardly wait until the next time.

And she knew in her heart there would be a next time. She'd been alone in the bed when she'd awakened this morning, but they hadn't needed to make promises. What they had shared had been too special to be expressed by mere words. She smiled to herself, realizing she was starting to think as romantically as Gideon spoke.

Mabel settled onto her stool and snapped her paper open. "Hah. I'm glad that banker cancelled. Someone's car blew up on the interstate south of Portland last night."

"What?"

"They figure it was biker gangs. There's a picture of the crater it left in the pavement."

"That's awful. Was anyone hurt?"

"No, seems the driver got out before the explosion, but the traffic's going to be murder while they fix that hole." She flipped to another page. "Here we go. Another day, another article on that Achilles bastard. It says they're making more progress."

Brooke cleaned off the pan and refilled her pastry

bag. She hummed to herself as she started to squeeze out another batch.

"Maybe that's what all of Trevor's hush-hush FBI business is about," Mabel continued. "Wouldn't that be a kick if they were tracking Achilles right in our backyard?"

"I suppose."

"Brooke, are you feeling all right?"

"I'm feeling absolutely wonderful, Mabel."

"I read you bad news, you've burned your eclairs and you're singing."

"Not really singing. Mozart didn't write any words."

"Mozart?"

Brooke hummed a snatch of melody from the "Rondo Alla Turca." "Catchy, isn't it?"

Mabel chuckled. "Now I *know* I should be worried about you."

"You were right yesterday." Brooke squeezed out another row of pastry shells, then paused to look at her friend. "I have been too focused on my work."

Mabel peered at her over her glasses. "I'm always right, but what made you realize it?"

"Sometimes it's good to take a chance and try something new. Like the music and these eclairs." *And making love with a dark, brooding stranger,* she added to herself.

Except Gideon wasn't really a stranger. There might be details she still didn't know about him, but their intimacy had taken them beyond that. Besides, from what he'd told her, there were details about him that even *he* didn't know. He'd been separated from his family at an early age, and from the few terse comments he'd made about the people who had raised him, he'd never known a loving home.

The more she learned about him, the more she wanted to wrap him in her arms and take away the loneliness—and the anger—she saw in his gaze.

Oh, yes. There was anger. She'd sensed it from the very first moment she'd seen him as he'd walked from the shadows of the forest into a glow of demonic red. She'd seen it during his confrontation with Rudy. And if she was honest with herself, it was that dark undertone that gave his passion such an exciting edge.

But then, everyone had some degree of darkness inside them. How people chose to handle it was what determined their character.

She finished baking the final batch of shells without mishap and was halfway through filling the cooled ones when there was a sudden thumping from the back door.

Newsprint rustled as Mabel folded her paper. "Are we expecting a delivery?"

"No. Not until this afternoon." Brooke wiped her hands on her apron as she crossed the floor. "I'll see who it is," she said, her steps quick.

She told herself it wouldn't be Gideon so soon. He was probably as exhausted as she was. Still, she couldn't prevent the eager trip of her pulse as she reached for the lock. Maybe she could finish these pastries later. Much later.

She pushed open the door, a welcoming smile already on her lips.

But it wasn't Gideon's intense, pirate gaze that

greeted her, it was a good-natured smile reminiscent of a big friendly yellow Lab. Oh damn, Brooke thought, fighting to control her grin. How was she supposed to look at Trevor with a straight face after Mabel's far-too-accurate assessment of the day before?

"Morning, Brooke." Trevor took off his hat as he crossed the threshold. He looked past her to Mabel. "Morning, Mrs. MacKenzie. Do you have a few minutes?"

Mabel started to reply, then winked at Brooke and slid from her stool. "I was just leaving."

Brooke closed the door and shot her a frown. Evidently Mabel hadn't given up hopes of matchmaking her with the sheriff.

Before either of them could move, Trevor spoke up. "If you don't mind, I'd like you to stay, ma'am," he said. He brushed the snow from his shoulders and unbuttoned his coat but didn't remove it. "This is official business that concerns both of you."

"The only police business that I'd be concerned about is catching that bastard Achilles," Mabel said, flicking her hand against her newspaper. "What can we do to help? Need some rope? A good hanging tree?"

Trevor frowned. He worked his hat brim in his hands. "Mrs. MacKenzie…"

"I'm teasing you, Sheriff," Mabel said. "You know I'd prefer to shoot him."

He didn't appear amused. Brooke knew he took himself and his job very seriously. "What's up, Trevor?" she asked.

"I'm here to offer the Highway Grill some extra work."

Mabel slapped her paper against her leg. "Aha, let me guess. You want us to cut him up and make stew out of him."

"Mabel, that's sick," Brooke said. "You're lucky Trevor realizes you're joking."

Trevor regarded Mabel blankly. "I'm an officer of the law. I don't joke about mistreating suspects."

"Hmph. You'd probably report us for violating the health code if we really did cook him," Mabel said, as usual not knowing when to quit.

Trevor shifted his gaze to Brooke. A muscle in his jaw twitched. She suspected it was from irritation rather than humor. "I want to arrange some private catering," he said. "It would be three meals a day for about a week."

Brooke nodded. "Do you have a guest in the basement?"

There were three jail cells in the basement beneath the sheriff's office. They usually weren't occupied longer than the time it took to schedule a bail hearing or sleep off a bender. The serious cases were transferred to the more secure facilities in the state capital, but occasionally a prisoner remained in Redemption for several days. When that happened, the grill provided the meals, so Trevor's request wasn't unusual.

To Brooke's surprise, Trevor shook his head. "No," he said. "I'm arranging the meals for some people who are coming in from out of town. We're going to be working at my office."

"What people?" Mabel asked. "Your FBI buddies from Portland?"

Trevor drew himself up. "I can't say. All I can tell you is it's official business."

"Good God, don't tell me I'm right," Mabel murmured, her tone suddenly dead serious. "Is this really connected to Achilles?"

To Brooke, it was obvious Trevor was enjoying their attention. He wanted to impress both of them with the importance of his work. But she wasn't impressed. If his work was really that important, he shouldn't have been so ready to brag about it to everyone within earshot.

"I'm not at liberty to say," Trevor finally replied. "Will you be able to handle the orders?"

"Will your friends pay the usual premium?" Mabel asked.

"Certainly," Trevor said. "I'll let you know the details next week." He fiddled with his hat brim again. "That baking sure smells good, Brooke."

"Thank you."

"Are you doing anything on New Year's Eve? I thought we might go to the dance at the Legion hall."

Her stomach sank at the sudden change of topic. She should have known it was coming—the years of compliments and clumsy flirtation had to be leading somewhere. Yet this was the first time Trevor had come right out and asked her directly for a date. She glanced at Mabel before she replied. "Sorry, Trevor. I'm going to be busy. I promised I'd work."

"I must have forgotten to tell you, Brooke," Mabel

said. "I've decided to close the grill at nine on New Year's Eve. Most people are at parties anyway."

Brooke restrained herself from throwing something at her friend. "I meant my own work. I'm sorry, Trevor."

He slapped his hat on his head and turned to the door. "No problem. I'll see you around."

The moment the latch clicked behind him, she whirled on Mabel.

Mabel held up her hands before she could say anything. "It's true. I actually did plan to close early. Why didn't you want to go out with Trevor? You might have had fun."

"I thought I explained that yesterday."

"From the way you've been so cheerful this morning, I'd assumed you'd changed your mind. You even said I was right. Do you really have anything better to do?"

Yes, I'm waiting for Gideon.

The thought made her pause. Waiting for Gideon was getting to be a habit. But she knew better than to base her happiness on any man, didn't she?

Oh, but Gideon was different. What they had was special, right? So sensual and romantic she had completely discarded her caution.

Then why hadn't he been the one to ask her out on New Year's Eve? It was only three days away. Why hadn't he left his phone number or asked for hers? Where did he live? Why didn't he drive a car? Why was she always trying to ignore or excuse the countless little weird things she noticed about him?

Even worse, why was she continuing to make excuses for all the things she *didn't* know about him?

She returned to the table, picked up the bowl of eclair filling and resumed her work in silence. Reality had begun to intrude, dimming the fairy-tale afterglow of the night before. She no longer felt like humming.

"So, do you think Trevor's out-of-town guests are from the FBI?" Mabel asked.

"Possibly."

"Aren't you curious to know what they're up to?"

"I'm sure we'll find out."

"If you put on some perfume and asked Trevor real nice, maybe—"

"Just stop it, okay? This is no longer funny." Brooke set the bowl down and braced her hands on the edge of the table. "I am never going to go out with the sheriff."

"Hearing bells isn't everything."

"It's not just because I'm not attracted to Trevor, it's because I don't want to get involved with a cop."

"Why not?"

"You know perfectly well why not."

Mabel studied her in silence for a moment. "If you mean what I think you do, you have to remember that was four years ago. Frank wouldn't—"

"I would never underestimate him. For all we know, Trevor's FBI friends could be tracking *me*."

"Brooke, no. That's a little farfetched."

"No more farfetched than believing they're after a legendary criminal like Achilles in Redemption."

Gideon sat at the mouth of the tunnel and watched the snow. The flakes were larger than the ones he'd seen the first time he'd come outside. Most were stopped by the boughs of the trees that crowded overhead, yet enough drifted to the ground to cover the tracks he'd made. In another few minutes, there would be no trace that anyone had come this way.

He held out his hand, catching a few snowflakes on his palm. They melted instantly, yet he couldn't prevent the shiver that shook his frame. His body temperature was elevated. His pulse was racing. Beads of sweat moistened his temples and his forehead. His vision alternated between excruciatingly clear and flashes of blurred white.

The symptoms had begun before he'd left Brooke's apartment. He'd likely hastened the onset by eating her food and drinking her water—and by repeatedly making love—but he'd wanted to experience every instant to its fullest.

The decision to return to the compound had been difficult, but in the end he'd concluded it was his only logical option. He would have preferred to remain with Brooke, but how could he do that to her? She had given him the best night of his life. He couldn't repay her by burdening her with his care as his health deteriorated. Worse, when he died, questions of his identity were bound to arise. If the Coalition discovered he'd been with Brooke, they would assume he'd confided in her. They would consider her a threat and want to ensure her silence.

For a while, he'd considered going somewhere else. There were infinitely more places in the world he wanted to go and things he wanted to experience. Yet how far could he get on foot with no money?

It was a fitting irony. The man who had stolen three hundred fifty billion dollars less than a year ago and had more personal wealth than he could spend in ten lifetimes didn't have a penny in his pocket. It was in his bank accounts in Switzerland. It was in the stocks and real estate he owned through his personal numbered companies that were hidden in the subsidiaries of Redcom Systems. It was in the priceless stolen art that hung on the walls of his quarters, the solid gold fixtures, the antique furniture, the heirloom carpets on the floors and rare first editions in the bookcases.

In the end, it was his wealth that had led to his decision to return. He needed to be here in order to access it.

He wiped the sweat from his forehead on his sleeve and pushed to his feet. Keeping one hand against the rock wall for balance, he made his way through the mountain to his quarters. He restored the live video feed and went through the charade of his morning routine, striving to appear as normal as possible. He didn't want to arouse suspicions now. He had little usable time left. It was only a matter of hours before his mind would cease to function. He had to work fast, but where could he start?

Perhaps his brain was already beginning to fail. Why else would he feel this smothering wave of conscience after so many years of keeping it at bay? Despite the throbbing pressure he felt building in his skull, the clarity of perception he'd experienced after making love with Brooke was strengthening. He might have left behind her modest apartment and Redemption's streets of unfinished homes, but with each step he had taken, he remembered every one of his crimes.

The impact Achilles had made on the world couldn't be erased as easily as the falling snow would be erasing Gideon's footprints. It was too late to reverse what he'd done. There was no time even to begin to right the countless wrongs. The best he could hope for was to make one person's pain easier to bear.

Gideon settled in front of his main computer, blinking hard to clear his vision. He angled his chair so that the camera in the ceiling wouldn't pick up the tremor in his hands as his fingers worked over the keyboard. He knew someone from the Coalition would be monitoring what he did whenever he accessed an outside computer, but that didn't trouble him. He was supposed to be working on the stock-market project, so they would expect him to access banks and other financial institutions.

He located the record of Brooke's loan application in the archives of the failed Redemption Savings and Loan. The sum was so modest, his remorse only deepened. But he didn't have time for the luxury of guilt. He needed to devote his full attention to setting up the maze of cyberspace traps and blind alleys that would enable him to safely give Brooke her dream.

A cramp knifed through his stomach. He clenched his teeth and completed the line of code he was inputting. The next thing he knew, he was lying on the floor beside his chair.

"Gideon?"

It was Willard Croft's voice, sounding as if it were

coming from an echo chamber. "What do you want?" Gideon muttered.

"Are you all right?"

"Yes."

"My assistant told me he saw you fall off your chair."

"I dropped my pen. It rolled under the table." Gideon got to his knees, fighting a wave of nausea. Only his years of training at hiding his feelings enabled him to pretend nothing was wrong.

"Do you need help?" Croft asked.

Even past the buzzing in his ears, Gideon clearly discerned the grudging tone of Croft's offer. Good. That would mean Croft was unlikely to pursue it.

Gideon inhaled through his teeth, then grasped the arm of the chair and levered himself to his feet. "No. Unlike the rest of you who prefer to do everything by committee, I am perfectly capable of retrieving a writing implement on my own, Willard."

There was a silence. Gideon imagined Croft was trying hard to restrain himself from snapping a sarcastic retort. He decided to give him a push. "Nothing to say, Will?"

"No."

"That reminds me, where's my Van Gogh?"

"Your…" There was a muttered oath. "I thought Oliver told you we're working on that."

Gideon squinted at the keyboard, hit the sequence of keys that would encrypt his work and turned away. "Let me know when you have it."

"But—"

"I'm through for the day. Now that you've seen fit

to interrupt me for no good reason, I'm going to take a nap.''

He hung onto consciousness long enough to reach his bed and hit the video control that would replay one of the nighttime loops he'd programmed. He couldn't let the Coalition learn what was happening yet. He needed to buy more time. Maybe if he rested for a few minutes he'd rally enough strength to finish.

Gideon awoke to clammy sheets, dried sweat and overwhelming thirst. He rolled from the bed and staggered to the shower room. Blood pounded behind his eyes with each step he took, but he gritted his teeth and dunked his head under the nearest spigot. Cool water sluiced over his neck and down his back, kicking his heart into a stuttering rhythm. He sank to the floor, the marble cold and slick against his skin.

Dimly, he marvelled that he was still mobile. How long would it last? He cupped his hands under the shower spray and drank until the tightness in his throat began to ease. The fluid revived him enough to enable him to shut off the water and crawl to the towel rack before the shivering set in.

The remainder of the day was a blur of violent, kaleidoscoping nightmares whenever he closed his eyes. Gunshots and blood. Panic. Loss. Pain. Gideon lost track of how many times he blacked out. At one point the shaking in his limbs grew so severe he could do nothing but curl into a ball so he wouldn't injure himself and hope for the spell to pass.

It did pass. By midnight, the tremors had tapered off to brief spasms in his muscles. He made full use of the reprieve by putting in an appearance at his computer again and picking another argument with Croft. He went through the motions of eating the food that was delivered, but he disposed of it the moment he angled himself beyond the range of the cameras. He had no appetite. He felt hollow, as if his body were being turned inside out. All he wanted to consume was water. Not the chilled bottled water that was supplied with his meal but the unlimited, punishing, cleansing spray from the shower.

This wasn't what he'd been told to expect. Gideon had studied enough about the human body to know the symptoms he exhibited didn't match those of an immune response. Granted, his condition was as unique as he was and thus impossible to predict with accuracy, but his DNA was still human enough for him to display some similarities to the clinically recorded characteristics of tissue rejection.

It made no sense.

Neither did the very fact that his mind was clear enough for him to *realize* it made no sense. The gamma-aminobutyric acid that was circulating through his brain should be deadening his synaptic activity.

But Gideon didn't want to squander what might be his final period of lucidity by analyzing it. He focused his attention on completing his work. By the evening of the second day, his manipulation of cyber records had created an untraceable bank account and a fictitious trucker from Washington who had named the Highway Grill and Brooke Carter in his will. The will was being probated in Seattle. The amount Brooke would shortly inherit wouldn't be enough to attract attention, yet it would be plenty to finance her bakery.

It was a small thing, as insignificant—yet as price-less—as one pure flake of snow drifting down to kiss a pockmarked battlefield.

He showered, quenched his thirst and fell into bed, expecting not to awaken again. Yet by dawn he was fully conscious. Despite the persistent feeling of hollowness and exhaustion, ideas were sparking through his brain. He rubbed his face and noticed that his hands were almost steady. He inhaled deeply and realized his lungs were as clear as his head.

It still didn't make any sense.

His heart pounding, Gideon slid out of bed and walked down the hall to his library. His muscles were stiff, his joints grated like broken glass as he moved, but his balance had improved. He squinted against the brightness of the chandeliers that illuminated the room. The newly acquired Renoir glowed from the wall, its dabs of color swirling like a captive butterfly. He waited for everything to steady, then climbed the spiral staircase that led to the upper gallery.

The effort stole his breath. He panted and leaned against the railing until the weakness passed before he made his way to the section that held his collection of medical texts.

It took him two hours to confirm the sum of his symptoms did not match any observed case of blood incompatibility, tissue rejection, allergic reaction or immune disorder. So he approached the problem from the other direction. He searched his books for a disorder that matched his symptoms.

It wasn't difficult to find. In fact, apart from the speed with which he was recovering, he was what could be called a textbook case. The irregular heart rate, the nightmares, chills and muscle spasms, the thirst and loss of appetite were all typically exhibited by addicts who were going through sudden narcotic withdrawal. Extremely unpleasant, but depending on the drug and the accustomed dose, in most cases not fatal.

Gideon replaced the books carefully, descended the stairs and sat in his favorite leather armchair. His breath was coming in short, sharp bursts. The sparks in his brain were turning to flashes of lightning, bolts of insight searing through the darkness. He felt brittle, stripped bare, his mind balanced on a knife edge. The thoughts he was glimpsing were so huge, they were painful.

Not an immune response. He had no immune response. He'd been exposed to blood, saliva and other body fluids from two different normal human beings and he had not reacted. He had not died. Instead, he appeared to be quitting drugs cold turkey.

What drugs? When? How?

He thought of Brooke's pastry and immediately dismissed it as a possible source. An addiction took months, years to be established. He'd felt as if his mind had begun to clear when he'd been with her, so how…

The answer was obvious. Whatever drug or drugs he was withdrawing from had to have been in his food. His specially prepared food…food that he hadn't touched in three days. The only food he'd dared to eat because if he had even a taste of anything else he would surely die.

Don't ever forget you can't eat or drink anything outside the safety of these walls, Gideon. You can't let anyone touch you. Only we can keep you alive.

But he hadn't died. Therefore, he had no fatal genetically engineered flaw. The isolation and special food had another purpose entirely.

The scope of the deception was challenging to grasp. It was brilliant. Self-perpetuating. As long as he ate the food, he wouldn't question the need to eat the food because of the mind-numbing effects of whatever drugs were in it. He hadn't questioned his life because it was the only reality he'd known.

The drugs had to be psychotropic. Something to make him compliant. Content. Were the drugs responsible for the holes in his memory? Was that why some part of him had been so determined to seek the truth? Why at times he'd felt as if he were losing his mind?

It fit. It all fit. His grasp of reality had been chemically veiled. His perception of reality had been based on a faulty premise. He had never suspected the truth because the lie had been so big.

The lie had been so big.

The lie.

He had been drugged.

He had been duped.

He had been kept isolated in a cage and manipulated into believing he had to steal to stay alive when all along he could have walked out the door at any time.

Gideon heard a succession of dull pops. He looked down. He was gripping the arms of his chair so tightly his fingers had pierced the leather. A scream was building in his chest. Haze descended on his vision, but it wasn't from any drug, it was from rage.

He had stolen billions for the Coalition.

In return, they had stolen his life.

Eight

Sometimes it was easier if you didn't look too closely at someone you cared about, Brooke thought. That way, there was less risk of not liking what you saw. Maybe that was why she had so readily overcome her caution in order to have a passionate affair with a stranger. The fewer the facts, the simpler it was to make excuses.

Brooke yanked her car door closed and turned her key in the ignition. She stared through the windshield at the jet engine that loomed at the edge of the Taber Aviation parking lot. The bulky metal cylinder gleamed solidly on its pedestal, the sleek casing illuminated against the night by the series of floodlights around the base. It had become a landmark of sorts in Redemption. As a matter of fact, a week and a half ago she'd used it to give a stranger directions.

But Taber Aviation was deserted. According to the security guard at the main entrance, the place had been shut down for more than a week. No one except a few of the company's top executives had been in during the holidays, none of them named Gideon Faulkner and none of them fitting his description.

Still, Gideon had only started working here recently. Maybe he was too new for the guard to have met. Or maybe he had a key to some other entrance and hadn't needed to ask the guard to let him in.

Brooke flipped the heater on high, hoping the noise of the blower would kick her thoughts back toward reality. Even now, she was trying to find excuses. She hadn't come here purposely to check out Gideon's story. He'd told her he'd had to work over Christmas, so she'd thought he might have had to work New Year's too. She'd wanted to see him, talk to him, give him a chance to explain why he hadn't contacted her.

Because Gideon had had plenty of opportunity to contact her. He knew where she lived, he knew where she worked. She was in the Redemption phone book. Surely even an egghead like him could figure out how to use a phone book.

But Brooke was through making excuses. She would have to be a fool to cling to her illusions in the face of the facts. Obviously, Gideon had lied. He didn't work at Taber. She probably wouldn't see him again. His pretty words had been a ploy to get her into bed. His method of seduction was unique and very effective, but the mind-blowing lovemaking they had shared couldn't have meant as much to him as it had to her. Otherwise, he wouldn't have disappeared without a word.

But what about his loneliness and his heart-melting need? What about the sense of connection she'd felt? Could it really have been only an illusion? She peered past the gleaming jet engine to the darkness beyond, half hoping he would appear out of nowhere as he had before.

"Stop it," she muttered. "Don't be pathetic."

She jammed her car into gear, her tires slipping briefly on the damp pavement before they caught. She forced herself to calm down before she turned onto the street. She was angry with herself more than with Gideon. She had let her heart overrule her mind and had dared to believe in…

Believe in what? Fairy tales? Love at first sight? Happily ever after?

It must have been the time of year, she thought as she drove past houses decked with glittering Christmas lights. Everyone got sentimental around the holidays. Considering the hours she'd been working, she likely hadn't been thinking straight.

And considering Gideon's knowledge when it came to lovemaking, there probably wasn't a woman alive who would be in any condition to think coherently after spending the night with a man like that.

Brooke gritted her teeth. Now she was making excuses for herself. But she knew better than that, didn't she? Excuses were just another form of denial.

Her anger had faded by the time she climbed the stairs to her apartment, leaving a hollow disappointment in its place. It might be easier not to look too closely at someone you cared about, but not looking at all led to disaster. Perhaps it was just as well things had ended this way. No relationship could survive if it was based on lies.

Besides, she was continuing to prove that she didn't need a man to be happy. She had come a long way on her own. Aside from her continued poor judgment when it came to romance, her life was going just fine. The eclairs she'd delivered to the mayor's reception had generated several inquiries. Her business was growing. At this rate, she'd—

Her thoughts came to an abrupt halt when she spotted the tall figure leaning against her door. His black overcoat hung open. His hair was a wild tangle on his shoulders. His entire frame seemed to pulse with a restless, leashed power.

Despite what she'd told herself and what she'd just learned, she couldn't prevent the eager leap of her pulse. Damn him. "Gideon?"

He straightened up when he saw her. He didn't smile. He didn't say a word. Instead, he strode forward, grasped her by the shoulders and hauled her against him. His breath hitched as he pressed his face to her neck.

For a startled moment, she swayed into his embrace. All he had to do was touch her and her common sense began to dissolve. She fisted her hands on his chest to keep from reaching for him. "Gideon, stop."

"Why?"

Damn him. There were so many reasons. She'd just been through them. But she could hear raw need grating through his voice and her body was already responding to the familiar feel of his.

He cupped her cheeks in his palms, tilting her face so she met his gaze. "Don't send me away, Brooke."

She might have summoned the strength to refuse, but then she saw his face. Dark circles tinged the skin beneath his eyes and his cheeks looked sunken, as if he hadn't eaten or slept since he'd left her three days ago. The common sense and resolve she'd taken three days to muster was swept aside by concern. "Gideon, what's wrong?"

He laughed. Or at least, he made a sound that could have been taken for a laugh if it hadn't been so cynical. "Everything but you, Brooke."

She touched his jaw. Black stubble bristled against her fingertips. "Are you ill?"

"No. I'm not ill. I'm perfectly healthy. I'm so healthy it's almost unbelievable."

"You look terrible."

"Then we'll leave the lights off so you don't have to look at me." He pressed his forehead to hers. "Whatever you want. Name it and it's yours. Just let me hold you, Brooke."

"But—"

"Please." He shuddered. His voice dropped to a rasp. "Don't send me away. You're the only truth in my life."

Oh, damn. How was she supposed to be cautious and sensible when he said something like that? She unlocked her door and let him in.

She didn't have a chance to turn on the lights. The moment he crossed the threshold, Gideon kicked the door shut with his heel and pulled her into his arms. Then his mouth was on hers, slanting across her lips with a sudden possessiveness that made retreat impossible. Their coats hit the floor together. She toed off her boots and heard the muted clunks as he did the same.

Had she thought she'd tasted urgency the last time they had done this? The memory paled compared to what she felt now. The demand in his touch was so powerful, it was intoxicating. She heard a button pop from her blouse and felt the scrape of his teeth on her shoulder. He pulled up her skirt as he backed her against the door. Cool air and fine wool whispered against her thighs.

She shivered. Not from cold but from the thrill of his hunger. It was starting again, the spiral of need that only he could trigger. Why? What was it about this man that made her reason short-circuit?

He clamped his hands on her hips and rubbed his knee between her legs. The darkness in the room wasn't total. Enough light filtered through the living-room window from the street to etch his features in silver.

His jaw was hard. His gaze held none of the tenderness he'd wooed her with before. No, there was no gentleness. There was too much anger.

Brooke caught his face. "Gideon."

He lifted her, using his body to hold her against the door as he guided her legs around his waist. His nostrils flared. He looked like…a stranger.

She had a flash of uneasiness. She had known there was darkness inside him—it was part of what drew her to him. She wasn't sure she had the courage to see it unleashed. Her spiraling excitement faltered. "Gideon, slow down."

He bared his teeth. It wasn't a smile.

She twisted, trying to slip out of his grip, but his body was too big. She grasped his hair and gave him a quick shake. "Gideon, wait. Please. Not like this."

His chest heaved. The tendons in his neck stood out

in hard ridges. He closed his eyes and tipped back his head.

She brushed a kiss across his chin. "Not like this," she repeated. "We have time."

"Time," he said. His voice was rough, as hard as his body. "There's so much lost time to make up for."

"You're here now. It was only three days."

He made a harsh noise in his throat. He set her down and let her skirt fall over her thighs, then wrapped his arms around her and stepped back from the door. Holding her off the floor, he pressed his temple to hers and turned in a circle. "Only three days. It feels like an eternity."

"Why did you stay away?"

"I thought I had no choice. But I did have a choice, Brooke. All along, it was up to me."

"I don't understand."

"And I can't explain it." He nipped the lobe of her ear. "Not yet. Not until it's over."

"Until what's over? Gideon, tell me what's going on."

"I'd rather make love to you." Still holding her, he backed her toward the bedroom. "If you want to go slow, we'll go slow. I'll strip off your clothes one item at a time. One inch at a time. I'll touch your body with every part of mine that will bring you pleasure. There are so many different ways we can try. Tell me what you like."

This was how it had happened before. But she had to think. Yet how could she think? Through the layers of fabric that separated them, she could feel his erection rub against her with each step he took. She remembered how he'd made her quiver. Her response was building anew. She was already anticipating how good it would be. Another night of bliss.

And then another three days of doubts?

She grabbed the bedroom doorway before he could carry her through. "Gideon, stop."

"What do you need?" He set her on her feet and splayed his hands over her buttocks. "Anything. Tell me."

"We need to talk."

"Later."

"Is sex all you want from me?"

"Brooke—"

"I thought we had something special. I thought it was beautiful."

"It was. It is. Trust what you felt."

"Trust?" She pushed out of his embrace and slipped past him to the hall. "I'd like to trust you, Gideon, but how can I when you lied?"

He reached for her, but she shook her head and stepped back. He closed his hand on empty air and dropped his arm. "I haven't lied to you, Brooke."

She turned around and walked to the living room, straightening her clothes as she went. She could hear his footsteps behind her, but she didn't look at him until she had switched on the lamp beside the couch. It was high time to see him clearly, whether or not she liked what she saw. "You did lie to me, Gideon. You lied about working at Taber. I went there tonight hoping to meet up with you."

He clenched his jaw. The hollows in his cheeks deepened. "Who did you talk to?"

''The security guard at the front desk. Why?''

''Did you tell him my name?''

''How else was I supposed to look for you?''

He regarded her in silence. His shoulders were rigid, his body vibrating with tension. He paced across the room to the front window and brushed aside the curtain to look down at the street. ''I didn't lie. I never told you I was employed at Taber Aviation,'' he said. ''You assumed I was because I asked you for directions.''

Was that true? She tried to remember, then realized it didn't matter. Even if he hadn't technically lied, he'd deliberately let her make the wrong assumption. ''You're playing word games.''

''This is no game, Brooke.'' He ran his fingers along the edge of the curtain, then withdrew his hand to let the fabric swing back into place. He turned to face her. ''I can't tell you everything, but I can tell you this. I went to Taber to use their computers in my search for information about my siblings.''

His siblings. The family he had been separated from in childhood. The children he remembered playing with on the beach. Brooke had a sudden urge to hold him. She crossed her arms over her chest and sat on the arm of the couch. ''All right, if you don't work at Taber, what do you do for a living?''

An echo of the anger he'd brought into the apartment with him flashed through his gaze. It was followed immediately by a spasm of pain. He looked at his hands. ''Most of my worth has been acquired through my inventions. Among other things, I design security devices for Redcom Systems.''

"I figured you had to be some kind of scientist. So you work at Redcom instead of Taber. Why didn't you tell me that in the first place?"

"I didn't want to drag you into my problems because I was concerned you might do exactly what you did tonight. It's better if no one knows we're involved." His hands curled into fists. "It was selfish of me to come here when I'm not free, but I had to see you, touch you, fill my lungs with your scent."

"Why shouldn't I be involved with you? What problems do you…" The word he used finally registered. "Wait a minute. What do you mean, you're not free?"

"There are…complications I need to deal with."

"Are you married? Is that it?"

His gaze snapped to hers. He appeared genuinely startled. "Brooke—"

"That's it, isn't it?"

He crossed the floor to the couch in three swift strides. "No."

"I'm an idiot. Pathetic. I should have realized there was a simple explanation."

He reached for her. "Brooke, please, listen to me."

She slapped his hand aside and jumped to her feet. She walked to the other end of the couch, putting the length of the coffee table between them. "It's so obvious now. That's why you were so mysterious and wouldn't give me your phone number. You were worried your wife might answer."

"I'm not married, Brooke." He rounded the table, his gaze steady on hers. "I have no wife."

"Is this another one of your word games? If you have a girlfriend or a fiancée or—"

"There is no other woman." He stopped when his toes nudged hers. He made a motion as if he were going to reach for her again, then raked his fingers through his hair in a quick, frustrated jerk. "There has never been another woman."

"Never? We only met ten days ago."

"Never, Brooke."

She let that pass. He couldn't have meant it the way it sounded. No man could make love as spectacularly as Gideon without some amount of practice. Not unless he was not only a fast learner but a superhuman genius. "Then what are these complications you're talking about?" she asked. "Talk to me, Gideon. Give me a reason to go with my heart instead of my head, because the more you say, the more I'm thinking the smart thing for me to do would be to throw you out."

"Yes, that would be the smart thing to do. I was taught that acting on emotion isn't rational. Emotion is a weakness. It can blind you to the truth and leave you vulnerable to your enemies. There is no profit in emotion. No logic." He leaned toward her, bringing his face to hers. "I can think of no logical reason for you to let me stay, Brooke."

That wasn't the answer she wanted. "Then maybe you should go."

He turned away abruptly but he didn't leave. He prowled the room, his movements laced with restlessness. "For more than twenty years I acted logically upon the facts I believed I knew. I focused on my work and my own survival and locked away my emotions because I thought they would make me weak. But if I had behaved logically, I wouldn't have returned to the Highway Grill. I wouldn't have touched you. I would still be alone.'' On his next circuit of the room he stopped in front of her and caught her wrist. ''Therefore, the best decision of my life was based on emotion, not logic. I acted on what I felt.'' He lifted her hand and pressed her palm to his cheek. ''I beg you to do the same.''

She should pull away from his touch. She couldn't. Although his cheek was rough from his unshaved beard, his caress was gentle. And his gaze, oh, his gaze was brimming with need. He was once more showing her the man she'd first met, the lost soul who haunted her. ''Why were you so angry when you got here, Gideon?''

''Because I discovered I was lied to.''

''By whom?''

''By the people who raised me. They shaped my entire view of reality, but it was all a lie. I thought I was in control but I deluded myself. They used me. They made me their victim and I let them.'' He wove his fingers between hers. ''I let them, Brooke. That's the worst part. My anger isn't only for them, it's for me.''

His words struck a chord. She remembered how she had felt in the parking .lot with Rudy. She hadn't wanted to be a victim. She hadn't wanted to feel powerless.

And beneath that memory lay another. A darker, older memory of the time she'd let Frank make her a victim.

She studied Gideon's gaunt expression, his tangled hair, the bleak frustration in his gaze. She recognized that look. It was the expression of someone who had come to a crossroads, someone who had been forced to face the truth of their life and didn't like what they saw.

It was a look she'd seen in the mirror four years ago.

She drew in her breath. Was this why she had felt a connection between them? It seemed so unlikely. She wouldn't expect a man as strong and smart as Gideon to let anyone take advantage of him.

Yet she knew better than most that given the right circumstances, the right strings to pull, anyone could be vulnerable. Anyone could be used. Abuse wasn't always physical. It could be emotional or psychological. The forms that victimization could take were as varied as people's capacity for evil.

Was this the real source of the bond she'd sensed between her and Gideon from the start? Was this why she had felt his loneliness, why she had overlooked common sense and behaved as if he weren't really a stranger?

Brooke's heart shouted the answer. It took her brain a bit longer to catch up. When it did, she felt a wave of guilt.

How could she stand in judgment of Gideon when she had lied to him herself? How could she expect trust and honesty when she hadn't given him either?

No relationship could survive if it was based on lies. Isn't that what she'd thought tonight just moments before she'd found Gideon on her doorstep?

But did she want a relationship with Gideon?

Of course, she did. There was no point fighting it any longer. Her feelings were just too strong. Even if she didn't believe in love at first sight, something irreversible had happened between them the night they had spent together. The connection was more than physical. She could no more turn her back on him now than she could have locked him out in the snow ten days ago. "What did they do to you, Gideon?"

"They lied about what I am."

"I don't understand. Does this have something to do with your adoption? Or that block on your memories of your birth family?"

"Yes, I suspect it's all linked. It's a complex situation. It's been difficult for me to uncover the truth because I not only live with these people, I work for them."

"You work for them? Are you saying your adoptive parents work at Redcom Systems, too?"

"It's more than that. They're among the people who founded it and continue to control it."

"Good God," she murmured. "They must be millionaires."

"Money has given them power. The place we live has every luxury imaginable, but it's like a fortress. A cage. That's why I haven't wanted you to contact me, Brooke. I don't want you exposed to them. And I don't want them to know how important you are to me."

"You make it sound so horrible. Maybe you should go to a lawyer or the police, no matter how powerful your parents are."

"No. Believe me, the police wouldn't be able to help me. I have to deal with this on my own."

"I wish there was some way I could help." She stroked his cheek. "You don't have to go back to them. You can stay here until you find somewhere else to live."

"Oh, Brooke." He pressed his mouth to her knuckles. "I would like nothing better than to stay with you, but I have to go back and sort this out or I'll never be free. What you've already done for me is unfathomable. You're my truth."

She winced. She slipped her hand from his grasp and stepped back. "I want to trust you, Gideon."

"You can, Brooke. I would never hurt you."

"But it's a two-way street."

"I'm not sure what you mean."

"I haven't been fair. If I want you to be honest with me, I have to do the same."

He smiled. "I've felt your honesty, Brooke. I've tasted it. It pulses through my body with each beat of my heart."

"Could you please stop the poetry for a minute? You're making this harder."

"I don't understand."

"I lied to you."

Gideon started. "What?"

"The last time we were together, when you asked me my name, I lied. My real name is Pritchard, not Carter. My given name is Brooke, but I took my last name from a sign on the side of the truck that brought me to Redemption. Carter's Haulage, that's what it said. It was a Kenworth carrying a load of dishwashers and microwave ovens to Eugene.'' She wiped her palms on her skirt. She knew what she was about to tell him might change everything, but now that she had started, she had a reckless urge to go on, to make a clean breast of it, to show Gideon it was safe to confide in her.

Yet this wasn't only for Gideon's sake. It was for hers. She wanted to prove to him—and herself—that it was all right to look closely at her, too.

''The driver stopped for dinner at the Highway Grill,'' she continued. ''I had run out of money by that time. That's why I had to hitch. Mabel gave me a meal and a place to sleep with no questions asked, in exchange for some baking.''

He rubbed his face, then pinched his cheeks and stared at her. ''Why did you change your name?''

''I was running away. It seemed a good way not to be found.''

''Why?''

She hesitated. ''You keep saying I'm kind and good, but you don't know the truth.''

''What truth?''

''I'm wanted by the law in Kansas. You see, Gideon, I'm a thief.''

Nine

If there were gods, they must be laughing, Gideon thought. Yet he felt no amusement. Instead, he felt humbled.

He understood the power Brooke had just given him. By revealing her secret, she was demonstrating her trust more clearly than any declaration could have. He could use the knowledge to gain control over her. That was what the people in the Coalition would do. Yes, they would capitalize on any sign of weakness or vulnerability and twist it to their own ends.

He'd been so wrapped up in his own crisis when he'd come here tonight, he hadn't given enough thought to how it would affect Brooke. He had to remind himself he was no longer alone. With each word he said, each move he made, the consequences of his actions spread outward like ripples in an ever-expanding pool.

He had much to learn about normal relationships. But he could think of no better teacher than Brooke. "Whatever you did," he said, "I'm positive that you believed you had no other choice."

She returned to the couch and sank onto the corner cushion. "No, I'm sure there was another choice, I just didn't see it."

"I understand how you feel."

"Yes, I think you do. That's why I decided to tell you."

He stepped over the coffee table and sat on the couch beside her, his thigh pressing firmly against hers. The contact produced a rush of warmth that had nothing to do with the arousal that still throbbed through his body. This was another kind of intimacy, this sharing of thoughts. It was an aspect of closeness he'd discovered he enjoyed almost as much as the physical. "I would be honored if you'd confide in me, Brooke."

"Honored," she repeated. The corners of her eyes lifted in a smile. "Oh, Gideon, you're something else."

That was true. Exactly what, he still wasn't sure. "Was the bakery that you told me about where your mother worked in Kansas?" he asked.

She tilted her head as she looked at him. "I nerve myself up to tell you I'm a thief, and that's your first question? Aren't you going to ask what I stole?"

"That's immaterial. I believe what matters to you is what drove you to it. You were happy when you lived with your mother, weren't you?"

"Oh, yeah. My mom worked long hours, but she always managed to make time for the two of us. And you were right, the bakery was in Kansas. Wichita, to be exact."

"Tell me about her, Brooke."

"But she has nothing to do with—"

"I disagree. I've only begun to realize that the past

explains the present. I want to know about all of your past, not just the part you were running from.''

"Okay, you asked for it. My mom was only seventeen when I was born. My father ran off when he discovered she was pregnant, so she had to quit school so she could support us. She never complained. She made me feel as if I was a gift instead of a burden.''

He had a sudden flash of a face. A dark-haired woman with blue eyes. The woman who had loaned her reproductive system to Code Proteus. That was how Agnes had described her, but he knew better now than to trust anything the Coalition said. He had to verify everything he'd been told, no matter how small—or huge—the fact. "She sounds like a wonderful woman, Brooke. I can see you inherited the nobility of her character.''

Her chin trembled. "Oh, great," she murmured, pulling her hand from his. She reached into a pocket on the side of her skirt and took out a folded tissue. "Now look what you've done.''

Concerned, he moved back to give her more space. What *had* he done? "I'm sorry, Brooke.''

"You never say what I expect. But it's okay." She wiped her eyes. "I guess seeing you look so upset tonight has stirred up a lot of stuff I had pushed to the back of my mind. The feelings kind of snuck up on me.''

"I'm sorry I caused you distress. But if it will make you feel better to talk, I want very much to listen.''

"It's hard to explain. Sure, my mother and I had our disagreements, especially when I was a teenager, but underneath it all was this solid foundation of love for each other that we never had to question.''

Love. What was that like? Gideon wondered. If he'd ever known love, he couldn't remember it. He moved closer to Brooke and slipped his arm around her shoulders. ''When did she die?''

''How did you guess?''

''Knowing you, nothing could have made you leave her if she was still alive.''

Brooke jammed the tissue against her eyes. ''You did it again.''

''I'm sorry. Whatever I did I—''

''No, Gideon. Don't apologize. It does make me feel better to talk. You're right. I wouldn't have left her. She wanted me to, though.''

''Why?''

She took a steadying breath and crumpled the tissue into a ball. ''This is going to sound like something out of a bad country-music song, but I don't want your pity. Everyone has their troubles. I don't consider myself special.''

''I would like to disagree and say that I believe you are special, but I'm afraid that might make you cry again.''

She gave a soft laugh, then leaned against his arm and dropped her head back into the angle between his shoulder and his neck. ''Okay, here's the short version. I won a scholarship to the state college the same year my mom was diagnosed with breast cancer. She was furious with me for turning down the opportunity of getting an education so that I could stay with her, but she needed me, Gideon. I took over her job at the bakery to keep a roof over our heads.''

Gideon stroked his hand down her hair, sifting the ends of her curls through his fingers. In a few simple words, Brooke was sketching a poignant picture of self-sacrifice and quiet courage. What would it be like to love someone that deeply, to be motivated by love instead of hate or greed or ambition? The concept was foreign to him.

Brooke sighed. ''This is where the story gets ugly. The bakery was owned by a man named Frank Schomburg. He was so understanding and supportive at first, I didn't want to look too closely to see what he was really like. He loaned me money to help pay for my mother's care. After she died, he invited me to move in with him. He acted so caring and sympathetic, and I felt so lost, I agreed to marry him.''

At the thought of another man with Brooke, Gideon felt a stab of unpleasant emotion. It must be jealousy. He thrust it aside. ''Did you marry him?''

''No.''

When she didn't continue, Gideon put the pieces together himself. ''He recognized your vulnerability,'' he murmured. ''He saw your love for your mother as a weakness and used it to gain control over you. Financially and emotionally.''

''Yes. That's exactly what he did. I knew you'd understand.''

''Do you still want to talk about it?''

''Oh, why not.'' She pushed out of his embrace and knelt on the cushion to face him. ''I've gone this far, you might as well know the rest. It's an all-too-common story. I felt dependent on Frank for food, shelter and affection, and because he had control of me, he felt free to use me for a punching bag.''

Something primitive and white-hot surged through his vision. If Frank Schomburg were here right now, Gideon knew he would kill him. He ran his fingertips over the delicate lines of Brooke's face. How could anyone want to hurt this woman? She'd done nothing. She was totally blameless. He didn't trust his voice, so he merely shook his head.

She leaned into his touch. ''It's like you said. The worst part is that I let him. He made me his victim, and I let him. For years. I don't think I'll ever get over the anger completely. That's why I can relate to what you're going through now, Gideon. I understand what it feels like to be betrayed and taken advantage of by someone close to you. Whatever happened to you, you can tell me, you can trust me.''

For a crazy moment, he wanted to do just that. He could see that his silence was causing a strain between them, but until he found a way to handle his situation, he couldn't involve Brooke in it. ''How—'' He had to clear his throat, his voice was too rough. ''How did you stop it? How did you break free?''

She glanced away. ''One day I woke up in the hospital. I guess the shock of that made me take a good look at my life. I didn't even think of calling the cops—I wanted to prove to myself I could handle it alone. The day I left the hospital, I went to the bank and cleaned out our joint accounts, then snuck into the office Frank had in the back of the bakery and smashed the lock on his strongbox. He had squirrelled away most of his cash there to hide it from the IRS. I didn't even stop to count it. I stole every last cent.''

"Good.''

"No, it wasn't good. I knew it was wrong, but all I could think of was hitting him where it hurt. That's why I took his money. Then I took his spare keys from the pegboard in the kitchen and stole his car so he wouldn't be able to chase me. Before I left Wichita, I gave all his money to a shelter for abused women, then I started heading west until the car ran out of gas. I left it at the side of the highway, hitched a ride with a trucker heading to Oregon and the rest you already know.''

Gideon reflected on what she had said. The similarities to his own situation were too glaring to ignore.

But the differences were even bigger. Brooke was a good person. The crimes she had been driven to commit had hurt no one except the individual who deserved it. And she had succeeded in making a new life for herself. Instead of dwelling on the misfortunes that had befallen her, she had dealt out her own version of justice and had gone forward.

Then she had stirred up all her old pain in order to help him deal with his.

Out of all the people he could have possibly met on the first night he had come to Redemption, it was a strange twist of fate that had brought him to Brooke.

Or was it that strange?

Maybe the gods didn't always laugh.

From the street outside the front window there was a sudden honking. Gideon tensed and looked around.

Brooke put her hand on his knee and squeezed

gently. "That would be the neighborhood kids celebrating. It must be midnight already."

He returned his gaze to her face, surprised to see that she was smiling. "What?"

"Happy New Year, Gideon."

He hadn't realized what the date was. Of course. The old year had just ended, a new one was beginning. People would be celebrating the change. It was the traditional time for resolutions and fresh starts.

And he wanted a fresh start. He wanted it so fiercely he began to tremble. "Happy New Year, Brooke."

He couldn't think of anything more to say, so he gathered her into his arms and kissed her. His feelings for Brooke were changing, deepening with each moment that passed. He wished...

He wished the night would never end.

He wished they could stay like this forever.

He wished he was human.

He pulled her under him as he stretched out on the couch. The rage he'd brought with him when he'd first kissed her tonight still churned in the darkness. So he kept the light on while they made love.

The laboratory that was buried in the mountain deep beneath the head office of Redcom Systems was a research scientist's dream. No expense had been spared. Along the right wall was an array of fume hoods, airtight Plexiglas cabinets where work was done through the thick rubber gloves that were attached to the front panels. Beside these was a long bench filled with glassware, everything from simple test tubes and petri dishes to complex vacuum-distilling equipment. In the center of the floor sat a large table that held analytical instruments such as an amino-acid sequencer, a gas chromatograph and electronic balances. The left wall of the lab held cabinets for chemical storage, a climate-controlled facility for culture storage, and the doorway that led to a room-size, state-of-the-art scanning electron microscope.

At the far end of the laboratory were individual work stations, L-shaped desks designed to accommodate each researcher's computer, optical microscope, laboratory manuals, notes, records and whatever else might be necessary to the project. One work station was larger, with the bench and desk surfaces slightly elevated from the rest. It was at this one that Agnes Payne sat.

Oliver Grimble pushed his hands into the pockets of his white lab coat and moved to stand behind his wife's chair. "How does it look?"

Agnes adjusted the focus of the microscope she was using. She replied without looking up from the eyepiece. "The cell culture isn't progressing as rapidly as we had calculated."

"Do you see any change at all?"

"Only minimal."

"Perhaps the tray I prepared yesterday will yield better results."

"I think your calculations were wrong again, Oliver."

"They weren't my numbers," he said. "They were Henry's."

Agnes swiveled her chair away from the microscope and skewered Oliver with a look. "You've hidden behind that excuse for more than twenty years. I'm out of patience."

"The cipher Henry used to encode his notes is difficult to translate."

"He wasn't that smart, Oliver. If he was, he would be here instead of us. I want you to recalculate those projections of the cell-division rate."

"Of course." He started toward his desk, then paused and cleared his throat.

"Is there something else?"

"Have you noticed how much Gideon seems to be sleeping lately?"

Agnes turned back to the microscope. "No, Oliver, I haven't."

"Willard mentioned it to me before he left for Arizona yesterday. He said Gideon has been spending more time in his bed than at his computer."

"I hope he hasn't let Gideon provoke him into saying something imprudent again. We've wasted three of our best men trying to steal that Van Gogh because of his last slip."

"No, Willard swears he didn't say anything to antagonize him. He only wanted to alert me to a possible problem."

She scowled, removed the slide she had been studying from the microscope's viewing tray and inserted another. "I'm pleased to hear Willard followed my advice and elected not to go to Portland. Victor is capable of handling the situation with Jake Ingram on his own. We need Willard to oversee the work on the new compound. More than half our personnel have already moved there."

"But what should we do about Gideon?"

"We might have to make arrangements to accommodate him in Arizona after all." She leaned over the eyepiece. "But if you want to help solve the problem of Gideon permanently, then give me correct calculations so that we can breed another one."

Oliver nodded, but Agnes wasn't watching him. He walked to the desk adjacent to hers and sat in front of the bench that held his computer. He called up a file of numbers, input them into the equation he'd devised earlier and waited for it to formulate the three-dimensional display. While the computer worked, he glanced at the video monitor that flickered on the low shelf separating his work station from Agnes's.

The image was almost completely black, except for a ghostly outline of carved bedposts and the hint of a recumbent figure.

"There," Oliver exclaimed. "He's sleeping again."

"What?"

"Gideon. He's dimmed the lights in his quarters."

Agnes swiveled away from her microscope with a loud sigh. She studied the monitor. "Yes, it appears you're right, Oliver."

"It's nearly noon. Do you think he's ill?"

"I doubt it."

"But Willard did mention Gideon appeared dizzy a few days ago."

"Gideon isn't ill. The dizziness and fatigue he's exhibiting are to be expected."

"I don't understand."

"We increased his dosage to ensure he remains compliant, remember? Even with his exceptional metabolism, he's going to have some side-effects until he adjusts to the new drug levels.''

"So that's all it is? Well, that's a relief.''

Agnes lifted her eyebrows. "Don't tell me you're feeling sentimental.''

"No, of course not. I just didn't want to go through the farce of suiting up to enter his quarters and check on him.''

"Yes, that is getting tiresome.'' She gave a sharp laugh. "It has worked well, though, hasn't it?''

"Indeed.'' Oliver leaned across the shelf between them. "You're a brilliant woman, Agnes. I'm eager for the day when you can get the recognition you deserve.''

She reached out to run a fingernail down the back of his hand. "So am I, Oliver. So am I.'' She nodded her head toward the dark monitor. "Perhaps we should wake him. The sooner he completes his latest project, the sooner our plans will come to fruition.''

"But he was adamant he needed rest in order to work,'' Oliver said. "I wouldn't want to push him too far.''

"It might be good to remind him who holds the power.'' She took her hand from Oliver's and reached for the controls at the bottom of the monitor. "I believe I would enjoy that.''

"What if he demands another painting? It would cause a delay.''

For a moment she toyed with the switch that would open the circuit to the speakers before she moved her hand away with an airy gesture. "Yes, that would cause a delay we can't afford. I'll check on him later.

As long as I wake him under the guise of being concerned for his health, I can use the opportunity to strengthen my control over him."

Oliver smiled. "As I said before, Agnes, you're brilliant."

She cocked her head, regarding him with interest. "I believe it's time for lunch."

"Whatever your pleasure, my dear."

She stood up and held out her hand. "We'll have it served in our quarters. Are you coming, Oliver?"

He got to his feet, took her hand and tucked it into the crook of his elbow. Neither of them noticed that the door to the corridor wasn't latched when they reached it.

And neither of them looked back. So they didn't see the black-clad figure concealed in the shadows beneath the equipment table in the center of the lab.

Gideon waited until the door had closed and the electronic lock had reactivated before he uncoiled from his crouch. He held his breath and listened. When he could no longer hear the faint taps of Agnes's and Oliver's footsteps, he exhaled hard and looked at his clenched fists.

It seemed these days as if rage was his constant companion. He should have been able to overcome it by now. He'd known what his so-called caregivers were like. He'd believed he'd had no illusions of there being any affection. He'd understood the delicate balance of power in their relationship with him, and he'd played it to his full advantage.

But while he'd listened to their words as they had discussed him so callously, he'd wanted to strike out like a child in a fit of frustrated temper. Bang his fists on the floor. Smash the fortune-worth of instruments that rested on the table. Shout his defiance into their startled faces and curl his fingers around their throats to rob them of their lives the way they had stolen his.

Gideon took shallow, rapid breaths until the fury subsided. It wasn't yet the right time for a confrontation. He had to use his head, not his hands. That was the only way he would be able to learn precisely what he was up against. He wanted a fresh start, and breaking away from the Coalition wasn't going to be as simple as escaping from a Wichita baker.

Still, in principle his strategy would be similar to the one Brooke had used with Frank. Gideon intended to strike the Coalition swiftly and unexpectedly. He would hit them where it would hurt the most, neutralize their ability to mount a pursuit and then...

And then things would get challenging. If Coalition personnel were already relocating to a new compound, then the FBI must be closer than Gideon had thought. Even if he neutralized the Coalition, he'd still be a wanted man. Jake Ingram and the police were as much a threat to his freedom as the Coalition, and he had no intention of escaping one prison only to be locked in another.

Would Brooke be able to forgive him when she learned what he was? The best thing he could do for her would be to disappear and let her get on with the life she'd built instead of dragging her into his troubles. Yes, that would be the logical choice...but his decisions concerning Brooke had never been logical. He couldn't conceive of a future without her, yet once she knew the whole truth, would she still look at him with trust in her eyes? Would she understand? Or would her compassion turn to revulsion?

He had no right even to ask the questions yet. Not when he was measuring his freedom one night at a time.

He walked to the desks at the back of the room. His gaze fell on the monitor where the loop of video he'd programmed displayed his darkened bedroom. He'd been lucky this morning, but the ruse wouldn't work much longer. It was only a matter of time before Agnes or someone else decided their agenda took precedence over his sleep.

What would they do if they discovered he had tricked them? Part of him almost wished it would happen, just to rattle their conceit and prove he wasn't as gullible as they assumed. But any satisfaction he would gain from that would be short-lived.

He had to stay focused. The Coalition had extended their tentacles far beyond the limits of his individual situation. It wouldn't be enough to cut off only the part that affected him. If he wanted to be truly free of them he would have to destroy the entire beast.

A beast he had helped create.

Gideon braced himself against a surge of guilt as he looked around the lab his actions had financed. Now that the drugs were being flushed out of his system, there was no longer any chemical buffer over his conscience. He remembered in detail every illegal act he had committed.

But he could no more afford to indulge his guilt than he could afford to indulge his anger.

He sat down at Oliver's computer and scanned the open files. Of course, Gideon had already surmised they weren't working to solve his fatal genetic flaw of the missing amino acid because there was no fatal flaw. They had mentioned Henry's notes. They had to be referring to Henry Bloomfield, the scientist behind the Code Proteus project.

Agnes and Oliver weren't trying to solve the problem of the original project, they were trying to duplicate its result. It was so obvious now, how could Gideon have not seen it? Was that because his thought processes had been impeded by drugs? Quite possibly. Or he might not have seen it because he hadn't wanted to look. He had been their captive genius. Once they succeeded in producing more like him, his usefulness and his power would be at an end.

Gideon browsed through the rest of the recently used files on Oliver's hard drive. From the looks of things, he and Agnes weren't having much success with their research. That was good. There would be less chance he would miss something when he implemented the program that would destroy it.

He checked the time on the bottom of the computer screen. According to the schematic of the compound, Agnes and Oliver's quarters were on the same level as this laboratory and only about two hundred yards down an adjacent corridor. He wouldn't have much more time before they'd be back. He moved to Agnes's desk in order to access her computer—he'd deduced she would want to keep the most sensitive information within her control. It took him less than three minutes to prove his reasoning was correct.

Gideon allowed himself a tight smile of satisfaction. Agnes's need to dominate and feel in control had made her a meticulous record keeper. He had embezzled billions electronically by transferring funds into an untraceable cyberspace maze that had emptied into the Coalition's accounts. **He** hadn't concerned himself with where the money had gone after that. Agnes had. She had made lists of every transaction, every country that sheltered Coalition henchmen, every government official who had been bribed, every judge who had been bought, every law officer who had been paid off....

His smile dissolved as he began to grasp the size of the conspiracy. Even with his skills, how would he be able to bring down something this far-reaching?

Still, if the money could be transferred in, it could be transferred out. He took the disk he had brought with him from his pocket, inserted it into the computer and began copying the files. While the drive hummed, he turned his attention to Agnes's desk.

Her penchant for order extended to her work space. The tray of slides she had been studying was neatly aligned on a flat rubber pad. Her reference books, notebooks and laboratory manuals were shelved in order of descending size. Gideon selected a notebook at random, slid it from the shelf and flipped it open.

The pages were filled with details of gene-manipulation experiments recorded in Agnes's cramped handwriting. From the dates in the margins, the work had been done four years ago. Judging by what Gideon had overheard this morning, the project hadn't advanced significantly since then. He wondered briefly why Agnes would keep her notes in longhand rather than storing them on the computer, but then he remembered how she liked to keep her notebook at her elbow. She had a way of curling her knuckles over the paper while she wrote, as if she didn't want anyone to see it. She favored ballpoint pens and sometimes when she was annoyed she would press so hard the pen would break through the paper.

The computer signaled the copying of the files was complete. Gideon removed the disk and slipped it into his pocket, then returned his attention to the notebook.

Had he seen Agnes take notes during the meetings in the conference room? He didn't think so. Agnes would be too conscious of maintaining her control of the agenda to do anything as menial as taking notes. So why was he certain this was Agnes's handwriting? And how could he know her writing habits?

He ran his fingertips over the back of a page, tracing the ridges of the words. The sensation pricked something in the depths of his brain. Could he still read the words backwards? He used to entertain himself by reading her notes through the page when it had been his turn at the sessions....

"Pay attention, Gideon. You must convert the results of the logarithmic function into binary before you substitute the next set of variables into the equation."

Gideon clutched the marker in his fist and climbed onto the stool so he could reach the whiteboard at the front of the room. He could tell by the pinched sound of her voice that Aunt Agnes was getting impatient, so he decided he'd better not tell her that she'd made a mistake in the third line of her calculations. It would be easier for him to just work the whole thing through in his head.

"Gideon." Aunt Agnes tapped her notebook with her pen. "I'm waiting."

He uncapped the marker, wrinkling his nose at the smell of the ink. It was like the mediciny smell in the room where Uncle Oliver had his special sessions. Gideon didn't like those. He always felt sleepy afterward. "It's our birthdays today. I hope we have cake."

"Sentiment is a waste of valuable time," Aunt Agnes muttered.

"Chocolate's my favorite. It giggles in my mouth."

"You will not see your cake if you don't do as I say. Now get on with it."

Gideon curled his tongue against his upper lip while he concentrated on forming the numbers just right. If he pretended it was a game, most times it was fun. He liked the way the formulas in the engineering textbooks described how things worked. He liked the squeak of the marker, too. This one was red.

"Very good," Agnes said.

"Can I go now?"

"Yes, but don't be late tomorrow."

Gideon jumped off the stool and ran to the door. It opened before he reached it. A dark-haired woman stood on the threshold....

Voices sounded in the corridor. The electronic lock on the door hummed. The scanning mechanism would be analyzing the thumbprint....

The past tangled with the present. There was danger

on the other side of the door. Who was there? What would happen?

Gideon wrenched himself back to the here and now. Had that been a memory? A dream? It had been so vivid, he could still picture the face of the woman who waited for him. Violet Vaughn. His mother. He could feel his heart pounding. Was it from fear or from eagerness?

The lock clicked.

Gideon shook off the questions, shoved the notebook back on the shelf and raced to the room that held the electron microscope. He cleared the doorway just as he heard footsteps enter the lab. Agnes and Oliver had returned.

Aunt Agnes and Uncle Oliver.

If he was bad they would take him to the room that smelled like medicine and he wouldn't have any cake.

Someone was reciting a rhyme. He didn't like it. He wanted them to stop but his lips were forming the words along with them....

Gideon pressed the heels of his hands against his temples, forcing himself to remain in reality. He couldn't allow himself to get drawn into the memory or he would be caught here. He wasn't finished. He still had days of preparations in front of him, more information to gather and programming to complete.

Whatever was locked inside his head would have to stay there until he had time to let it out.

Ten

"There's nothing to be afraid of," Brooke said to herself. She gathered the bags that held the foil plates of food and bumped the car door closed with her hip. "You're just being paranoid."

The Redemption sheriff's office was on the main street. It was a redbrick single-story building that adjoined the town's post office. Aside from Trevor's Bronco with the light bar on top, the collection of cars and pickups that were angled into the parking spaces on this side of the street probably belonged to people who were picking up their mail. Still, Brooke couldn't help checking the licence plates as she walked past.

She was reassured when she saw that none were from Kansas.

The front room of the sheriff's office was separated from the entrance by a wooden counter and an old-fashioned wooden spindled gate. On the far side were two filing cabinets, a coat rack, a coffee machine and several desks. Most of the desks were empty, thanks to recent budget cuts that had led to the downsizing of the sheriff's department. Nancy Savard, one of the deputies who had hung on through the layoffs because she happened to be the mayor's daughter-in-law, was working at the computer on her desk. She waved when

Brooke came in, then turned to call over her shoulder. "Your order's here."

A strange man stood at the back of the room beside the frosted glass door that led to Trevor's private office. He wasn't wearing a uniform, but to Brooke it was obvious he was a law officer. His neat haircut, his impassive expression, his conservative gray suit, everything about him suggested cop. He crossed the floor smoothly. "Put the bags on the counter, please, ma'am."

Brooke did as he asked.

Instead of picking them up, the man opened each bag and looked inside. He took a pen from his suit pocket and used it to pry open the containers. His inspection was swift but thorough. When he was finished, he nodded his thanks to Brooke, carried the bags across the room and rapped on the frosted glass door.

The door opened. Another man with gelled hair and a dark suit took the bags. Before he could swing the door closed, Trevor emerged from the office. Trevor spoke quietly to the man who had been standing outside, waited until he had joined his companion in the office, then walked over to greet Brooke. "That dinner sure smells good, Brooke. You and Mabel outdid yourselves."

"Thank you." She noticed three shadows moving on the other side of the office door. "I brought four specials, just like you ordered. It was roast beef and baked potatoes today."

"Did you bring any of your pie?"

"Yes. Apple cranberry."

"Great." He straightened the cuffs of his uniform and cleared his throat. "I hope you didn't work too hard over New Year's."

"I need to work hard to get my business going." Hoping to deflect the conversation away from the subject of New Year's—and the tentative overture Trevor had made the last time she'd seen him—Brooke took the bill Mabel had prepared from her coat pocket and put it on the counter. "Mabel would like you to pay this in cash."

He frowned. "I'll sign the bill and settle up later."

"Sorry. Mabel insisted on cash. You know how she is."

"Fine." He turned toward his deputy. "Nancy, would you take care of this? I need to get back to the meeting."

"Sure, Trevor." Deputy Savard pushed away from her desk and went to one of the filing cabinets. "We wouldn't want Mrs. MacKenzie to charge you interest the way she did last year."

Trevor gave Brooke a tight smile and returned to his office. As soon as he'd gone inside, the man who had first greeted Brooke took up his previous post outside the door.

Yes, his post, Brooke thought. It was obvious to her that he was guarding that door. And he'd gone through the bags of food she'd brought as if he were looking for explosives. Who else was in that office? For once it seemed that Trevor hadn't been exaggerating the importance of his job. Something serious was going on here.

"What was the total?"

Brooke shifted her attention to Nancy. She was crouching over the lowest drawer of the filing cabinet, a small steel cash box open in front of her. Brooke read out the figure at the bottom of the bill.

Nancy whistled softly. "That Mabel has some balls."

"She warned the sheriff there would be a markup."

"Well, if the food's halfway as good as those eclairs you brought to Dad's reception last week, it'll be worth it." She closed the box, shoved the drawer closed and carried the money to Brooke. "Besides, the government will cover it."

Brooke leaned over the counter and lowered her voice. "What's going on, Nancy?"

She pursed her lips. "They won't tell me."

"But the suits are FBI, right?"

"I really can't say, Brooke."

"Does this have something to do with that bombing in Portland? The papers said that involved biker gangs."

"Your guess is as good as mine."

"I sure hope they don't come here," Brooke said, glancing out the front window. "Redemption can be a rough place, but at least we don't have anything as bad as that."

Most of the tables were filled when Brooke returned to the grill. Now that the holidays were over, business was picking up. Phil and Paul sat among a group of truckers near the door, gossiping and cramming down their food by turns. Work on the highway improvement project on the edge of town had resumed yesterday, so several men from the construction crew occupied the stools at the counter.

Mabel stood by the cash register, snapping lids on a pair of large coffees for a weary-looking young couple. "Take care on the road," she said to them. "If you're sleepy, for God's sake, pull over."

The man couldn't have been out of his teens. He counted out a pile of change on the counter as the girl picked up the coffee cups and a small paper bag. "Thanks," he said. "We will."

Mabel pushed the coins back to him. "The coffee and muffins are free today."

The young man flushed. For a moment he seemed as if he wanted to protest her charity, but then he scooped up the money and stuffed it back in his pocket. With his arm around the girl, he started for the door.

"Use the money to get a haircut before you go to that interview," Mabel called after him.

Brooke smiled. That was just like Mabel, demanding an outrageous sum from Trevor and then giving out free food along with advice when the mood suited her. "Okay, what did I miss?" she asked.

Mabel shrugged. "The kid's looking for work."

"Uh-huh. You're such a marshmallow."

"We need more muffins."

Brooke laughed. "I'll get on it first thing tomorrow. Who needs serving?"

"I'm caught up except for the spooky guy in the far corner."

Brooke grabbed her order pad and headed for the customer Mabel had indicated. Her boss was right—

this man definitely looked spooky. Not mysterious or intriguing the way Gideon was, but almost…creepy. He was as wiry as a scarecrow and had a face like a skull. Despite the noise of the restaurant, he seemed to surround himself with a pocket of stillness. Dead air.

She took out her pen. "Hi. What can I get for you?"

He closed the plastic-coated menu he'd been holding and looked at her. His eyes were set so deeply in their sockets they didn't appear to have any white around the irises. "I saw no salads on your menu."

"Our customers don't usually ask for any, but I can fix one up for you if you like."

"That would be fine. I heard your establishment delivers."

Brooke didn't like to judge people on appearance, but his stare was making her uncomfortable. "Not usually."

"I'm not often mistaken. Someone mentioned that you had gone to the sheriff's office."

Was she being paranoid again, or was he trying to pump her for information? She took the menu and tucked it under her arm. "Really? Huh, imagine that. Would you like your salad to go, then?"

He nodded slowly and turned his gaze to the window. From where he sat, he had a good view of her car.

A thin strip of light was glowing beneath the door of Brooke's apartment when she arrived home that night. She wasn't alarmed—since she had given Gideon a spare key, he had been waiting for her every night. The first time he'd brought her a CD with a compilation of Chopin's waltzes. The night after that, he'd brought her an old, leather-bound volume of poetry by John Keats. They found a surprising amount to talk about, even though he spoke little about himself. Then again, sometimes they didn't talk at all. Yesterday, he'd scooped her off her feet when she'd stepped over the threshold, opened her coat and had made love to her right there on the floor.

He was as intense as ever, an exciting, sensitive lover. Their intimacy was deepening with each night they spent together, as if he truly was trying to make up for lost time. The hurt and anger she'd seen in him last week were gradually being replaced by resolve. He might not be ready to confide the details of his troubles with his adoptive parents, but he was making it easy for her to be patient.

She still didn't regret her decision to confess her past to Gideon. It had felt good to tell the truth, and to be accepted as she was.

"Gideon?" she called as she opened the door.

"I'm in the kitchen, Brooke. You're home early."

"Uh-huh. Mabel closed early to celebrate getting the government to cough up a hundred and forty bucks for four blue plate specials." She took off her coat and followed his voice to the alcove at the edge of the living room. She didn't see him at first, but then she spotted the top of his head. He had moved her refrigerator away from its spot in the corner beside the stove and had squeezed himself into the space behind it. "What on earth are you doing?" she asked.

''This machine wasn't running properly,'' he replied.

''Yes, I know. I just give it a kick when it acts up.'' She set the bag of food she'd brought from the grill for him on top of the stove, then stretched forward so she could see him better.

Gideon was stripped to the waist, bent double as he squatted on the floor. His hair was held by a black cord at the nape of his neck and hung between his shoulderblades. His skin gleamed with a moist film from exertion, and black smudges that looked like grease streaked his forearms. The muscles in his upper arms and shoulders corded as he bent a piece of copper tubing into a tight spiral.

The sight of him half-naked made Brooke's stomach dance. He had a magnificent body and appeared completely unselfconscious about displaying it. She'd never met a man who was so oblivious to the way he looked. She allowed herself a moment to enjoy the view, then lifted on her toes so that she could see the back of the fridge. ''Good God,'' she murmured. ''You took the thing apart.''

''I didn't take it apart entirely.'' He fitted the tubing to a metal box the size of his fist and inserted it all into a gaping hole halfway up the fridge. Using a screwdriver, he fastened a metal plate over the hole. ''I only needed to make a few adjustments so I could install a device to improve the operation.''

''Uh, don't take this the wrong way, but have you ever fixed a fridge before?''

''No, but the principal of the mechanism wasn't difficult to understand.'' He twisted to insert the electric plug into the socket on the wall behind him.

The motor started up with a soft click, made a noise closer to a whisper than a hum and then shut off.

Brooke grimaced. ''It was old anyway,'' she said. ''Maybe I can call the landlord to send someone over to get it working.''

Gideon picked up the wires and the screwdriver and climbed out from behind the fridge. He dropped the leftover parts into a bag, replaced the screwdriver in the drawer where she kept her odds and ends and maneuvered the fridge back into place. ''It is working, Brooke,'' he said, opening the door. The light came on and a puff of cold air rolled over her. ''It sounds different because I modified the windings around the central power plant to enhance the isentropic compression of the refrigerant so it draws less electricity to exhibit the same thermodynamic properties.''

She didn't understand half of what he'd said, but she could feel for herself that the appliance was working better than it ever had. It shouldn't surprise her— he'd told her that he was an inventor, so he was bound to be handy.

The motor did another brief whisper. Gideon closed the door. ''If it doesn't please you, I'll restore it to the way it was.''

She shook her head and smiled. She brushed a stray lock of hair from his forehead and tucked it behind his ear, then moistened a towel with some dish soap and started wiping the grease from his arms. ''I was wondering how you'd top Chopin and Keats. How are you with cars? Mine's due for an oil change and a tuneup.''

"I would be happy to look at it.''

"Maybe when you're wearing more clothes.'' She ran her fingers along his biceps. "You know you don't have to do things for me. And you don't have to bring me presents, either.''

"I want to. I don't think you realize how important it is for me to know I'm welcome here, Brooke.''

"Oh, I think I do. Mabel was there for me when I needed a place to sort things out. It feels good to be able to pass the favor on.''

He placed his hands on her hips and drew her closer. "You're like no one I've known, Brooke. Your generosity continues to amaze me.''

She moved the towel to his chest. There was only a small spot of oil there, but she enjoyed the excuse to rub her hand over his muscles. "You're pretty unique yourself.'' She paused, her gaze caught by a streak of white beneath the scattering of crisp black hair. "What's this?''

"What?''

She ran her fingertips over a puckered ridge of skin. "I can't believe I never noticed this before. How did you get it?''

"I had surgery when I was ten.''

"It must have been serious. This is right over your heart. What happened?''

"I'm not certain. I no longer trust the version I was told, and my memories are hazy.''

She pressed a kiss to his chest. "Well, I think it looks sexy.''

He laughed. It was a wonderful sound, deep and rich and over too soon. "Only you could find a positive side to something so ugly."

"It's a part of you, Gideon. It can't possibly be ugly."

He kissed the tip of her nose and eased away. "I have another present for you."

She turned as he walked past her. He went to the small round table beside the wall in the living room where they had eaten breakfast together before dawn this morning. Papers covered the top. Some were filled with what appeared to be lines of mathematical equations, others held sketched diagrams. She hung the towel on the handle of the oven door and followed him to take a closer look. "What's all this?"

"It documents what I did to your refrigerator." He selected several papers from the pile and stacked them together. "According to these calculations, the appliance will now draw ninety-two point seven percent less electricity. The diagrams illustrate how the modification can be duplicated and installed on other appliances. I've listed several reputable companies who would likely be interested in manufacturing and marketing the device. Once you apply for a patent—"

"Whoa. Wait a minute here. Are you saying I could sell that gizmo you stuck in my fridge?"

"Other people would do the selling. They would have to pay you for the rights since you would own the patent. A good lawyer should be able to negotiate at least twenty million up front and a share of the profits."

Brooke's knees gave. She pulled out a chair and sat down. "You're kidding, right?"

"The figure may be wrong. It could be closer to sixty. I'm more familiar with security devices than with energy conservation, but with the cost of power escalating, I believe there would be considerable demand for this…gizmo."

She stared at the papers in his hand. "If that contraption really works, it would be worth a fortune."

He held out the papers to her.

Her heart thumped. She moistened her lips. "Gideon, why would you give me this?"

"Because I have nothing else I can offer you."

"Offer me? I told you I don't expect presents."

"I've taken so much from you, Brooke, and given so little in return. I wanted to make sure you'll never be in a position where you could be dependent on anyone."

"I'll be fine, Gideon. I don't have to be a millionaire to be happy. I'm on my way to starting up my own business. You should use the earnings from this invention yourself so you can—" She was struck by a sudden thought. "Oh, no. Do your parents have you tied up in some kind of financial agreement with Redcom Systems? Is that why you can't sell this invention on your own?"

"No, I don't need the money. Over the past few days I've changed the accounts where the earnings from my previous inventions are deposited so that I can access my funds without going through Redcom." He set the papers carefully on the table, then did a circuit of the room. "I'm preparing to leave my current position, Brooke."

"What are you going to do instead?"

"That depends on how successful my departure is." He continued to pace. "I'll be moving out of…my home as well. I won't be able to stay there once I quit."

"That makes sense. There are plenty of vacant apartments in Redemption because of all the layoffs."

He rubbed his face. "Yes. I know how difficult times have been here."

Her heart thumped again. "You're still welcome to move in with me, Gideon. I know it's probably not as fancy as you're used to, what with the money your adoptive parents must have, but you've been staying here every night anyway so—"

"I can't, Brooke." He detoured to the kitchen and picked up his discarded shirt. "I'm leaving Redemption."

She watched him as he shrugged on the garment. This one was of fine linen and cut loosely. A poet's shirt. Like the rest of his clothes, it was black. She wondered why he always wore black. Even though he looked great in black, he couldn't wear it out of vanity, since he wasn't vain.

And wondering about his wardrobe was easier than looking at the fact that he was leaving. "Are you saying goodbye? Is that why you wanted me to have this design?"

"I'm not saying goodbye." He started on the buttons. "I want you to have it in case something goes wrong."

"I don't understand."

He returned to where she sat and placed his hands on her shoulders. "Brooke, I'm more at ease with computers and mechanical designs than with people, so it's difficult for me to explain how I feel. You are the most precious aspect of my life. The hope of a future with you is what inspires me to sort through the tangle of my present."

"I still don't understand what you're getting at. You say you're leaving and then you say you want a future with me."

"Yes." He drew her to her feet. He clasped her head in his hands, stroking her temples with his thumbs, studying her face as if he were committing it to memory. "Both statements are true. When I leave Redemption I want you to come with me."

She caught the edges of his shirt. "What? Gideon, I have friends here, I'm starting a business. How can—"

"How can I ask you to give that up? I don't have the right to ask. I don't deserve even to hope, but that doesn't make any difference. My desire for you is beyond reason. Do you think this is love?"

"What?"

"The feeling between us. You've talked about love, and I've read about it, and I think I can see it in some pieces of art, but I don't remember whether I've ever known it." He lowered one hand to cup her breast through her sweater. "When we have sex, our bodies flow and meld into one, yet even when we don't touch, I feel as if we're joined. When I'm with you, I feel more alive. We're separate, and we can exist on our own, yet you've become necessary to me, like a part of me that makes me whole.'' He dipped his head and kissed her lower lip. ''You're always in my thoughts, like the echo of a melody or the rhythm of a poem, but I don't know what to call this. Could it be love?''

She didn't know how to reply. She'd been tiptoeing around that question herself for days. ''It's supposed to take longer,'' she said. ''To know for sure.''

''I thought emotion didn't follow rules.''

''It doesn't.''

''Then how can anyone know for sure?''

''You just do. You take it on trust.''

''I trust you with my life, Brooke. And I hadn't truly begun to live until I felt the touch of your skin against mine. This feeling that warms my soul very well could be love.''

She couldn't decide whether she wanted to laugh or cry. Hearing Gideon discuss love with his quirky combination of innocence and passion was pushing through every rational defense she had. It definitely was too soon. Yet she could think of no reason to object. ''I can't believe this conversation.''

He licked the tip of her ear, then nudged her hair aside with his nose and kissed the side of her neck. ''Why not?''

''You never say what I expect.'' She tipped her head to the side. ''And how can you talk while you're doing that thing to my neck with your tongue?''

He pulled up her sweater, undid her bra and rubbed his palms over her nipples. ''I've thought of some other things I can do with my tongue.''

She quivered. ''We still have to talk, Gideon.''

"Later. First I'll show—"

His words were drowned out by a sudden rapping on the apartment door.

Brooke wanted to ignore it. It was almost midnight. Whoever it was must have the wrong apartment. She swayed into Gideon's caress.

"Brooke Carter?" A man's voice, one she didn't recognize, came from the corridor. "Miss Carter, open the door."

Gideon stiffened. He lifted his head and dropped his hands to her waist.

There was another knock. "FBI," a different voice called. "Open the door, Miss Carter."

Gideon swore under his breath. "Not now," he muttered. "Damn, not now. All I need is one more day."

Brooke pushed herself away from Gideon. "Oh, God," she whispered, hooking her bra. "I wasn't being paranoid. Frank didn't give up. He must have sent them." She straightened her sweater and looked around the apartment, as if another way out would suddenly appear. She ran to the window and looked outside. A bubble of panic rose in her chest when she saw the Bronco with the light bar on top. "Oh, God! Trevor's out there too."

Gideon jogged to her bedroom and then her bathroom. His expression was stony when he returned. "There are police officers at the back of the building as well."

She grabbed his hand. "It's been four years but the statute of limitations is seven. I crossed state lines with Frank's car. I'm sorry. I thought I was safe."

"You are safe. Don't say anything more and you'll be fine." He gave her a swift kiss. "They called you Carter, not Pritchard."

"But—"

There was a loud thud. Wood splintered. The door crashed inward and men poured through the opening. They fanned out, their guns drawn.

Gideon moved in front of Brooke, putting his body between her and the weapons that were aimed at them. In a voice she'd only heard him use once before, a voice like honed steel, he said, "They're not here for you, Brooke. They're here for me."

Eleven

This had been Brooke's recurring nightmare. Having her past catch up with her, being taken into custody and interrogated by the police, that was the shadow that had hung over the new life she'd made in Redemption. Yet no one had mentioned Frank's money or his car. Instead, the nightmare was expanding into something far worse. "I don't believe you, Mr. Ingram." Brooke curled her fingers around the arms of the oak chair so no one would see that her hands were shaking. "It isn't possible."

"Miss Carter, the evidence is irrefutable," Jake Ingram said. He closed the frosted-glass door of Trevor's office behind him. Chair legs gritted across tile as he pulled up another chair beside hers. "The individual you know as Gideon Faulkner is in fact Achilles."

She wished she could view this as someone's idea of an extremely sick joke, but Jake Ingram sounded dead serious. He wasn't a cop—his suit was far too expensive-looking and well-tailored for that, and his hair wasn't styled with that cop-neatness of his colleagues. He claimed to be the special investigator who had been hired by the World Bank to coordinate the FBI's hunt for Achilles. Law officer or not, he had a piercing quality to his blue gaze that marked him as an intelligent and determined man.

Brooke shifted her attention to Trevor. He was sitting across from them behind his desk. He hadn't said much since he had torn her away from Gideon and put her in the back of his Bronco. Instead he'd been watching her with an expression of sad-eyed disappointment. "I don't believe you," she repeated.

"They've been zeroing in on Achilles's location for months," Trevor said. "Believe them."

"The papers have been full of stories to that effect all year, but I thought Mabel was right and it was all government propaganda." She returned her gaze to Ingram. "If the FBI really had been closing in, they wouldn't have let anyone know they were coming."

"That's very astute of you," Ingram said.

"And thanks to the way our sheriff has been talking and the way your pals so obviously look like feds," Brooke continued, "the whole town probably knows you people got here yesterday. Even some guy in the restaurant had heard something was up. If the real Achilles had been anywhere near Redemption, he would have been long gone by now."

Ingram looked at Trevor. "Who is Mabel?"

"She owns the Highway Grill, the restaurant that catered our dinner," Trevor replied. "And she regularly robs me blind."

Brooke sat forward to jab her finger at Trevor. "It's bad enough that you're slandering Gideon, but don't start accusing Mabel of anything. You might not appreciate her humor, but Mabel MacKenzie is a good businesswoman and has never hurt a soul in her life."

"You're very loyal to your friends," Ingram commented.

"That isn't a crime."

"It is when they're wanted for stealing three hundred fifty billion dollars like your new boyfriend," Trevor said. "Now I understand why you were too busy to go out with me. You were with Achilles all along. You can be charged with being an accessory, for harboring a fugitive, for—"

"Sheriff, please," Ingram interrupted. "This isn't helping."

Trevor folded his arms over his chest and tipped back his chair. "Go ahead then, Jake. It's your show."

Ingram turned back to Brooke. "Your friend Mabel was right, Miss Carter. The stories in the papers have been propaganda. So was our rather obvious arrival in Redemption."

"What do you mean?" Brooke asked.

"Achilles is part of a large criminal organization that has been thwarting our attempts to find him. We had to resort to using misinformation and decoys in order to draw the criminals out and pinpoint their location while we got our people in place."

"You mean you lied."

Ingram kept his gaze steady on hers. "Yes. We've been concentrating our resources on this area for weeks."

"If you lied before, why should I believe you now?"

"Because you are caught in the middle of a dangerous situation, Miss Carter. Only by cooperating with us can you guarantee your safety."

"The only guns I've seen so far belonged to you and your pals who broke down my door."

"Then you didn't see the plastic explosive we removed from your car."

She felt the breath whoosh from her lungs. The bravado and adrenaline that had gotten her through the past hour began to fade. She pressed herself back in her chair. "What?"

Ingram took a file from Trevor's desk, drew out a series of Polaroid photos and passed them to Brooke. "This is what we found before we moved in on your apartment."

She recognized her car. She didn't recognize the bundle of wires or the gray putty-like mass that was crammed beside the spare tire in her trunk. "Oh, my God," she whispered.

Ingram took another photo from the file and handed it to her. "Have you seen this man?"

The photograph appeared to have been taken at a distance. The resolution wasn't good, but the face was nevertheless identifiable. Gaunt cheeks, sunken eyes, a face like a skull. "Yes," she said. "I saw him at the grill. He ordered a salad. He knew I had made a delivery to the sheriff's office."

"His name is Victor Prego," Ingram said. He took the photos from her and returned them to the folder. "He has attempted to kill me several times since I began this investigation. Until he rigged your car, his most recent effort was a car bomb in Portland."

No, it wasn't a joke. This was definitely a nightmare. "I thought biker gangs were responsible for that car bomb."

"The explanation we gave the media was false."

"But why would this man want to harm me?"

"You weren't the target. I was. The explosive device in your car had a remote control detonator. We surmise Prego intended to wait until you were delivering the next order to the sheriff's office before he activated it. There was enough Semtex in the car to have flattened the entire building, the post office next door and most of the block."

She knotted her fists in her lap as she thought about what might have happened. "We all would have been killed. You and your friends, me, Nancy. Oh, God. The post office was full when I delivered dinner yesterday. There were families with children there."

"Which is why we wanted to have our people in place before we revealed our presence. We had Prego under surveillance and were one step ahead." Ingram moved to the edge of his chair and leaned one hand on the sheriff's desk, boxing her in. "This is also why we couldn't delay any longer before moving in on Achilles. We are dealing with a group of criminals who have proven themselves to be ruthless and without remorse, Miss Carter. They must be stopped, and so must Achilles."

Brooke shook her head back and forth in a slow denial. "You're wrong about Gideon. I trust him. He wouldn't hurt me or anyone else. He couldn't possibly be involved with people like this."

"He has been living with these people for over twenty years," Ingram said. "They raised him after he was separated from his family at the age of ten. Gideon Faulkner is a genius, a criminal mastermind.

His work as Achilles has financed the entire clandestine organization.''

''No.''

Ingram leaned closer. ''We have observed his excursions from the fortified compound beneath Redcom Systems for several days now. We followed him directly to your apartment. There is no doubt he is the man we are seeking.''

Brooke swallowed against the lump in her throat. ''No. Gideon couldn't be Achilles.''

''Have you seen where he lives, Miss Carter? Has he told you about his background? Didn't you ever wonder why you only see him at night?''

''He lives in one of those fancy places on the mountain,'' she said desperately. ''Gideon isn't a monster. He's thoughtful and sensitive and—''

''Didn't you wonder why he surrendered to us without a fight?''

Brooke pressed her hands to her eyes to hold back the tears. But she couldn't hold back her thoughts. Pieces were clicking into place and the picture that was forming was too horrible to take in.

They're not here for you. They're here for me.

No. Please, no. It couldn't be. Not her gentle Gideon with the lost-child longing…and the anger…and the darkness…and the bleakness on the night he'd come to her like someone who had been forced to face the truth of their life and didn't like what they saw…

The things Ingram was saying fit with what Gideon had told her. It all made a terrifying kind of sense.

Yet there were still huge pieces missing.

Brooke wiped her eyes and lifted her chin. Gideon

had given her the benefit of the doubt. He hadn't judged her. She could do no less for him. "Whatever you think he did," she said, echoing the words Gideon had once said to her, "I'm positive he believed he had no other choice."

Only a portion of the window was visible from Gideon's cell. The glass was covered by a steel mesh, set high on the cement-block wall. A streetlight in front of the building cast a pale gleam on the floor of the basement room. The sky beyond the lamp was black, but dawn was less than five hours away.

Gideon rested his forehead against the steel bars of the cell door and studied the lock. It was an old-fashioned mechanical device, not electronic. He didn't have much to work with—before he'd been put in this cell he'd been relieved of his belt, his boot laces and even the cord that he'd used to tie his hair. Still, it would be a simple matter for him to manipulate the tumblers in the lock by using the piece of loose wire he'd noticed behind the conduit under his cot. Once he disabled the guard, he could dismantle the frame of the cot and use it to pry the mesh from the window.

He shook back his hair and surveyed the room. There were two cells on each side, but his was the only one that was occupied. He looked at the man who was seated at a small metal desk beside the door to the stairs. Special Agent Lansky of the FBI stared back at him impassively. Gideon hadn't yet seen the man in charge. Jake Ingram was making him wait, probably hoping to gain an advantage for the upcoming interrogation.

Gideon returned his gaze to the window. He couldn't wait much longer. The more he delayed his return to the compound, the slimmer his chances of making it back undetected. The video loop in his quarters would run indefinitely, but as the day progressed, it was highly probable someone would decide to disturb him. He needed to get back in order to complete the program he'd started. He needed to access the compound's main computer system to implement it. Otherwise...

Otherwise he would never be free. He curled his fingers around the bars until his knuckles whitened. He had been so close. If he hadn't gone to visit Brooke tonight, he would have been able to complete his preemptive strike against the Coalition. His desire to see her hadn't been rational, yet he'd felt compelled to touch her, to make love to her, and to assure himself she would be all right even if he failed.

Emotion had made him vulnerable. It had left him open to attack and had allowed his enemies to trap him. And it was emotion, not these steel bars, that was keeping him here.

He couldn't escape until he was certain that Brooke was not going to be charged with any crime. He had to convince Ingram that she was innocent. He wanted her to have a future...even if she no longer wanted him in it.

There was a sharp rap on the stairwell door. Lansky got to his feet and looked through the narrow window that was set into the panels at eye level, then unlocked the door and swung it open. He spoke to someone outside for a few minutes, then turned in the doorway and called to Gideon. "You have a visitor, Achilles."

Gideon felt something tear loose inside him when he saw Brooke step over the threshold. He'd managed to maintain a veneer of calm until now, but the sight of her here among the dingy cells and the gray cement was more than wrong, it was obscene.

"Ten minutes," Lansky said, propping the staircase door open. "I'm going to be right outside so don't even think of trying anything stupid."

Brooke pressed her lips together and moved forward, her gaze too bright.

Gideon stretched his arm between the bars and held out his hand.

She gave a strangled cry and ran the rest of the way across the floor. She seized his hand. She didn't say anything. The questions were plain in her gaze.

He wove his fingers between hers, feeling her touch steady him. "Are you all right?" he asked.

She shook her head. A tear dropped on his knuckles.

"What happened? Did they hurt you?"

"No. They searched me, that's all. And they told me—" Her voice broke. She shook her head again.

"They told you that I'm Achilles."

She curled his hand to her breasts. "You said you haven't lied to me."

"I haven't."

"I don't care what evidence they have. If you tell me it isn't true, I'll believe you."

"I won't lie. It is true."

She exhaled hard and closed her eyes.

"Brooke, I'm sorry. I didn't want you to learn it

this way, but it was safer if you knew nothing until we could leave together. This way you can't be convicted of any crime." He stretched his other arm through the door so he could touch her hair. He rubbed a curl between his fingers, absorbing the texture, the scent, remembering how it had felt draped over his thighs. "Have you been charged?"

She moved her head from side to side.

"If you do need money for a lawyer, use the plans for the energy-saving device I've left you as collateral. I've taken steps to replace the money you lost when the Redemption Savings and Loan failed. You'll be hearing from another bank soon. So will your friend Mabel. I know it will never make up for—"

"Damn you," she muttered.

He faltered. "I'm sorry. I—"

"Damn you, Gideon!" She snapped her eyes open. "I've been alone for four years. I'd thought I was doing just fine and then you came along and all my common sense went out the window. Of all the men I could fall in love with, why did it have to be you?" She dropped his hand and slammed her palms against the cell door. "Damn! The whole world wants your head. My best friend would gladly shoot you. When were you planning on telling me?"

"When we were safe," he said. "When I had completed my plan to destroy the people I worked for so that I could cleanse some of the guilt that taints my hands. You said you love me."

"Of course, I love you. Why else would I have been such an idiot?"

He felt an unfamiliar prickling behind his eyes. It

was hot. Uncomfortable. He had to blink to clear his vision. "I thought it would take more time. To know for sure."

"We don't have time. Jake Ingram has given me ten minutes to convince you to make a deal."

"No deal."

"Wait. Hear me out. It's our only chance."

He looked at the circles of fatigue beneath her eyes and the pinched lines of worry at the edges of her mouth. "It is love. This pleasure and pain could be nothing else."

"Gideon—"

"I love you, Brooke."

She curled her fingers around the bars that separated them. "Don't turn poet on me again, Gideon, okay? Not now. I'm trying to find a way out of this mess."

He knew there was only one way out of his situation, but he was certain Brooke wouldn't agree with it. "All right. I'll listen."

"The FBI wants you to help them."

"How?"

"If you testify against the people you worked for, you'll serve a minimum sentence and then you can join me in the Witness Protection Program."

"Minimum sentence?"

"That's part of the deal."

He tamped down a burst of fury. He'd spent over twenty years in a prison that he could have left at any time. He didn't believe he could retain his sanity if he willingly submitted himself to a new set of jailers. "Not for a year. Not for another day. I can't."

"I'll wait for you, Gideon. We'll be given new identities. It's the only way we can be together."

He stroked the fingers she had curled around the bars, marvelling at the strength in her small frame. "You would be willing to give up the life you've built here?"

"I've done it before. It worked then and it can work again."

"It isn't the same, Brooke. Once the Coalition realizes I'm no longer under their control, they won't let me go. I'm too dangerous to them."

"Who's the Coalition?"

"That's what the people I worked for call themselves. I know how they operate. The network is too far-reaching."

"Ingram told me about the people who raised you. We'll be safe from them in the Witness Protection Program."

"Unless the entire organization is destroyed in one simultaneous strike, the FBI won't be able to protect us."

"Yes, they can. They're a step ahead this time. They found the bomb that Prego guy put in my car before it could be detonated."

Gideon clasped his hand over hers. "What?"

"It wasn't meant for me. It was meant for Jake Ingram when I delivered the next order from the grill. Gideon, let go, you're hurting me."

He released his grip and backed away from the cell door. He pivoted and paced to the back wall. It was only two strides, not nearly enough space to work off his outrage. He slammed the side of his fist into the cement.

"Gideon! Don't. You'll hurt yourself."

He thought about what could have happened to Brooke and hit the wall again. The guilt that roiled inside him was so strong, he couldn't breathe. Victor Prego was only one of the evils Gideon's crimes had fed. And Brooke, kind, generous, innocent Brooke, could have been killed simply because she was a means to an end.

What had he done all these years? What the hell had he done? His eyes were burning now. He wiped his face roughly with his sleeve. He had stopped stealing for the Coalition months ago, but the consequences of his deeds continued to spread. More ripples from his actions, expanding ever outward. "They have to be stopped. Whatever the cost."

"Then you'll take the deal?"

"That won't help."

"Sure it will. With your testimony, you can put them all in prison."

He turned to glance at the window. How much time did he have left?

"Gideon, your hand is bleeding."

He looked at his fist. Blood welled from a split in his skin and dripped on the floor. He welcomed the pain. It would help him focus. "I helped create the Coalition, Brooke. It's up to me to destroy them."

"The police—"

"The police don't have my capabilities. No one else does."

"They said you were a genius."

"That's right. I am."

She laughed shakily. "From anyone else that would sound conceited, but I know you. I've seen what you can do. Your mind works differently from mine."

"My mind *is* different. I'm unique. Only someone with my special skills can undo what I've done."

A man's voice came from the doorway. "I couldn't agree more."

Gideon turned. A tall stranger stood by the door to the stairs. His gaze was steady, his eyes vivid blue. Something flashed in Gideon's memory. A face, a voice. He blinked and it was gone.

"It will take someone with your skills to bring down the Coalition," the man said. "That's why I was assigned to the case."

Gideon struggled to pull his emotions back under control. He knew who this was. After months of a cyberspace chess game, he was finally face-to-face with his nemesis. "Jake Ingram, I presume."

The man nodded, stepped forward and swung the door closed behind him. He selected a key from the ring he carried, locked the door carefully and slipped the key ring into an inside pocket of his suit jacket. "And you are Achilles."

There was no point denying it. Gideon had larger concerns than that. "I prefer to be addressed as Gideon."

"That's fine with me. I never did like your nickname." Ingram propped one hip on the desk where Lansky had been sitting and regarded him from across the room. His gaze was as steady as his voice, but there was an undercurrent of excitement vibrating through his frame that belied his relaxed pose. "What made you choose it?"

This wasn't the interrogation Gideon had expected. It was an odd question. Even odder was the fact that he couldn't answer it. He didn't know why he had chosen to call himself Achilles. Perhaps that was one of the memories that had been blurred by drugs.

"Mr. Ingram," Brooke said. "Gideon needs a doctor. He's injured his hand."

"Slamming it into a brick wall will do that." Ingram twisted to the side to pull open the drawers of the desk. He withdrew a small white box with a red cross on the lid. "I take it you weren't careless enough to break any bones, were you, Gideon?"

Gideon flexed his fingers. No, he hadn't broken anything. If he had, it would have been more difficult to enter the final lines of code in the program he needed to complete.

Ingram set the box on the desk and looked through the contents. He withdrew a plastic bag of cotton balls, a bottle of antiseptic, a roll of gauze and a snub-nosed pair of bandage scissors. He held them out to Brooke. "Do you know anything about first aid?"

She nodded and crossed the room.

"Too bad my sister isn't here," Ingram said. "Faith is the medical expert in the family."

Brooke snatched the first-aid supplies and hurried back to Gideon. He returned to the cell door and extended his hand between the bars. While she cleaned and bandaged the split in his knuckles, he tried to keep his attention on Ingram. What strategy was the man using now? Was he trying to put him off guard? There was no logical reason for him to mention his sister.

"Now if Marcus were here, he might be more of a help to you, Gideon." Ingram's words were casual but his gaze was keen as he continued to regard him. "He could make a new door in those bars using nothing but his bare hands. He's the brawn of the family."

"I can't take your deal, Ingram," Gideon said. He turned his hand as Brooke wound the gauze over his palm. "I have to finish what I started."

"No, that's my job now. And call me Jake. Miss Carter, don't try to slip him those scissors. He's inventive enough to make a file out of them."

She used the scissors to clip the gauze and tucked the end of the bandage into itself. She carried the supplies back to the desk and dumped them into the box. "I don't know how you can make light of the situation," she said. "Gideon shouldn't even be here. He wants to stop these Coalition people as badly as you do."

"Yes, from what I overheard, he does. But then, he's a genius. He might have realized I would be listening and said what he thought I would want to hear."

Brooke propped her hands on her hips. "That's not true. He's been trying to break away from them since New Year's. They lied to him and used him. He thought he didn't have a choice."

"You stated you didn't know what he'd done," Ingram said.

"Not all of it, but—"

"Brooke, don't," Gideon said. "You're not involved in this, so don't say anything more."

She spun to face him. "The hell I'm not involved. I love you, Gideon. You might be locked away from me, but you're not alone anymore. There's no way I'm leaving you to go through this on your own."

Something else tore loose inside Gideon. The urge to take Brooke into his arms was so strong, he was aching inside. He had lived without love, without touch, for years. Now he couldn't imagine how he had.

Brooke's eyes filled as she looked at him. She started forward but Ingram caught her elbow to stop her. "Why did he think he had no choice?"

"Leave her alone, Ingram," Gideon said. "She doesn't know."

"Then you'd better tell us both," Ingram said. He released Brooke's arm and straightened up from the desk. His face hard with emotion held tightly in check, Ingram walked across the floor to stand directly in front of him. "Tell me why you stole three hundred fifty billion dollars and collapsed the world's economy, Gideon. Tell me why you used the gift of your genius to further the schemes of the Coalition for more than twenty years but now claim you've had a change of heart. Because despite who you are and despite what this woman who claims to love you wants me to believe—" He made a sharp gesture, the first crack he'd allowed in his control. "Despite what *I* want to believe, unless I get a good answer, twenty-five to life is the best I can offer you."

Gideon looked him square in the face. They were the same height. They had the same color hair and eyes. For a crazy instant Gideon felt as if he were looking in a mirror. "There's no point, Ingram. Your deal won't work."

"Gideon, please," Brooke said. "You both want the same thing. You want to stop the Coalition."

"Yes, we want the same thing," Gideon said, not moving his gaze from Ingram. "I need you to unlock this door and let me go now. That's the only way we can get it."

"Explain," Ingram said.

"I have records of where the money I stole went. Names, dates and bank accounts of every link in the Coalition's worldwide chain. I used this to devise a computer program that will hit every link simultaneously and make it impossible for the Coalition to access one penny of their wealth. Without wealth, they have no power. Their projects will collapse, their political protection will dissolve and the organization will self-destruct. Only then will your justice system be able to handle them."

"Give me the program," Ingram said. "I can implement it."

"You have proven yourself a worthy adversary," Gideon said. "I respect your capabilities, but they won't be enough to complete my work. I designed the Coalition computers. Only someone with my special abilities can manipulate them."

"Yes."

"Then let me go so I can do it."

Ingram didn't move, yet his body continued to pulse with tension. "Your argument is logical, except for one point."

"What?"

"There were five children in the Code Proteus project. They all have special abilities. You are not unique, Gideon."

Gideon hadn't anticipated this. He'd known Ingram was good, but he hadn't realized how good. How had the man put the facts together?

"The children were separated when the project was disbanded," Ingram said. "One of them—you, Gideon—was raised by Agnes Payne and Oliver Grimble. Together with other disillusioned scientists and ex-CIA agents, they established the organization known as the Coalition."

As Gideon continued to stare at him, he had another flash of memory. A boy with blue eyes, black hair and a teasing grin. He thrust his hands through the bars and grabbed Ingram by the lapels, jerking him against the cell door. "What do you know about the other children? Are they alive? Are they well? Where are they? Tell me."

Ingram caught Gideon's wrists but he didn't break his grip. He held on to Gideon as firmly as Gideon was holding on to him. "They're alive and thriving, even the sixth child we never knew about who was given away at birth. Connor is a technological genius who's overcome his blindness. Mark goes by Marcus now. He joined the navy and became a SEAL. Grace calls herself Gretchen. There isn't a puzzle or a code she can't solve. Faith went into medicine, as I mentioned before. As for your oldest brother, he had an extraordinary talent for numbers. He used it to make money. Legally."

Gideon sucked in his breath. Ingram said they were alive. They were fine. The names were familiar. Mark.

Grace. Faith. But Ingram had said *his* sister's name was Faith.

A woman's voice was calling. Gideon looked up from the water wheel as the tide flooded the channel he'd dug around his generator. "Gideon, time to come in. Mark, Grace, where are you?"

The shadows on the sand beside him moved as the children called in reply. Gideon gathered his toys, then scrambled to his feet and took Grace's hand. She squeezed it affectionately.

Mark slapped him on the shoulder and ran past them. "Race you to the house, Achilles! Last one there's a rotten egg."

Gideon laughed and started to run alongside Grace.

"Faith?" the woman called. "Where's Jake?"

A girl with long dark hair waved from the top of a dune and pointed down the beach. "He's right there, Mom!"

Gideon turned his head to see his brother sprinting across the sand after Mark. It would be a close race. Jake always hated to lose....

Grace, Faith, Mark and Jake. The children on the beach with him. His sisters and his...

"I'm your brother, Gideon," Ingram said.

Gideon didn't respond. He couldn't. His throat had closed. He looked at the face of the man on the other side of the bars. It melded with an image of a boy. His big brother. Jake.

Jake Ingram was his brother. He was alive. He was here.

And by keeping Gideon in jail, Jake would surely kill them all.

Twelve

How many shocks could a mind take before it snapped? Simply snapped? Brooke suspected she was drawing close to the limit. Why else would these crazy revelations seem to make so much sense?

She swayed on her feet, grabbing the edge of the steel desk for balance, then made her way hand-over-hand to the chair and sat. The men's voices echoed hollowly from the cell across the room as they continued to talk. She forced herself to concentrate.

Gideon was a thief. The most successful thief in history. Okay. She'd had a few hours to get used to the idea now and thought she could handle that, since she was no angel herself. She knew what people could be driven to do in order to survive. The difference in their crimes was only a matter of degree, right? He regretted what he'd done. He'd believed he'd had no choice. She was sure he was a good man inside.

Right. Fine. That much she could learn to deal with. But he wasn't just a man. He was a genetically-engineered superhuman from Code Proteus, the secret CIA experiment that had started back in the nineteen-sixties. It explained why she'd always felt he was...different. She'd heard about the Code Proteus children. The tabloids had had a field day when the story had broken last year. The rumors had ranged from disconcerting to ridiculous. Secret armies of supermen. Dangerous mutants. Freaks. Monsters.

Brooke had dismissed the stories. Remarkably, so had Mabel. They had been far more concerned with the news about Achilles.

But evidently the stories about genetically-engineered children had been true. She was looking at two of them. Now that she knew, it was easy to see the resemblance between the men. They had the same height and coloring, the same directness in their gazes and they both had that weird aura of intensity that set them apart.

Gideon had wanted to find his birth family. Well, it appeared that one of them had found him first. Too bad the first thing long-lost brother Jake had seen fit to do was to throw his little brother in jail.

The thought sent Brooke back to her feet. She took a moment to summon her strength, then crossed the room and grabbed Jake Ingram's arm. "Are you really Gideon's brother?"

He jerked, startled at the interruption. He released his grip on Gideon and looked at her. "I am."

Brooke gave his arm a shake. "Then where have you been all these years?" she demanded. "From the sound of it, the rest of you had happy, normal lives while Gideon got stuck with the parents from hell."

Gideon let go of Jake's jacket and stepped back from the door. "Brooke—"

"How dare you ask Gideon to explain what he did," she cried. "It's a miracle he turned out to be as fair-minded and sensitive as he is, considering the way he was raised by criminals. For God's sake, he was only ten when they got their hands on him. Why didn't the government keep track of these children? Why didn't anyone make sure Gideon was all right? As far as I'm concerned, you're the one with the explaining to do, not him.''

''It's complicated,'' Jake began.

''Oh, don't give me that,'' Brooke said. She wiped her cheeks, surprised to feel tears there. She hadn't even noticed that she was crying again. She reached through the bars and caught Gideon's injured hand. ''See the blood on this bandage? Now, I know I don't have your education or your IQ, but you two geniuses are thinking this thing to death. You're both as human as I am and sometimes we humans have to take things on faith. Or did the scientists in Code Proteus forget to engineer you a heart, Mr. Ingram?''

She could see by the flicker of pain on Jake's face that her jab had hit a nerve. She would apologize later. Right now her only concern was Gideon.

Jake slipped his hand inside his jacket to withdraw the ring of keys. He unlocked the cell door and swung it open. ''I can't let Gideon out,'' he said. ''Not until we settle on a deal. But I can let you in.''

Brooke was through the opening in a flash. She stepped into Gideon's embrace and locked her arms around his waist.

He laid his cheek against the top of her head, his breathing unsteady. ''Pleasure and pain,'' he murmured. ''Is love always like that?''

She hiccuped. ''Oh, Gideon. Not always. But sometimes love means you take the bad along with the good.''

The door clanged shut. Brooke heard the key grate in the lock. She burrowed her nose against Gideon's collar and hugged him more tightly.

Jake cleared his throat. ''Miss Carter is right, Gideon. I do owe you an explanation. Until last April, when you surfaced in cyberspace as Achilles, none of us knew you were alive. We didn't know who we were ourselves. Agnes Payne and Oliver Grimble had used drugs and post-hypnotic suggestion to block the memories of our childhood when Code Proteus was disbanded because they wanted to use us to further their schemes. Our mother managed to get everyone except you away from them, and she arranged private adoptions so the Coalition couldn't trace us. She wanted us to be safe from them even if it meant she'd never see us again.''

Brooke felt Gideon's chest rumble with the question that had come to her mind as well. ''Why was I the one who was left behind?'' he asked.

''You were shot. Our mother thought you were dead. Otherwise, she never would have left you.''

Brooke could feel a shudder work through Gideon's frame. He was silent for so long, she grew worried. She lifted her head to look at his face.

He stroked her cheek with his fingertips. The edge of his bandage caught in her hair. He focused on it as he worked it loose. ''That would be the scar you saw on my chest, Brooke.''

She thought of the puckered white ridge on his skin and remembered how close it had been to his heart.

She splayed her hand over his shirt, wishing someone could have been there to protect him. "You were only ten. You never had a chance."

"I remember the blood and the pain. The smell of gunpowder and violets."

Jake moved to the side of the cell where they stood. "Have your memories come back, then?" he asked.

Gideon replied without moving his gaze from Brooke. "Not completely. I have only glimpses. Agnes and Oliver told me my mother was the one who shot me on the orders of the government."

"Bastards," Jake muttered. "That isn't true. Agnes was the one who shot you."

Gideon moved his hand to the side of Brooke's neck. It wasn't so much a caress as a simple need for physical contact. "The deception must have begun immediately after the surgery to remove the bullet," Gideon said, shifting his gaze to Jake. "They would have needed to take precautions against infection so I would have been isolated and closely monitored. They likely realized the isolation would keep me contained and thus they came up with a reason to prolong it."

"What deception?" Jake asked.

Anger flared in Gideon's eyes. He looked around the cell, his jaw hard. "They told me I was flawed, that the same genetic alteration that gave me my genius would make contact with any normal human fatal."

Jake put his hands on the bars. "What?"

"They laced my food with drugs so that I wouldn't think to question the story and they made my prison a palace so I wouldn't leave. And I didn't. For two decades I believed the lie and did their bidding so that I would survive. I thought I would die if I left, either from an immune reaction or from a government assassin's bullet. I believed I wasn't fully human and so I touched no one. I thought I had no choice.'' His gaze returned to Brooke's and the anger faded. ''But then I met a woman who opened her heart to me and showed me what living really is.''

Brooke's mind was too shell-shocked. She didn't want to take in anything more. After all the other revelations, this one was simply too much. It couldn't be true. What kind of monsters would cold-bloodedly and systematically deprive a child or a man of freedom, of human contact, of the simple comfort of touch?

Oh, God. She had once asked Gideon what his adoptive parents had done to him. Now she almost wished she didn't know. Yes, the forms that abuse could take were as varied as people's capacity for evil, but not in her worst nightmares could she have imagined this horror. The last pieces of the puzzle that was Gideon were finally snicking into place. The misery he'd caused as Achilles was vast, but the wrong that had been done to him was beyond her comprehension.

She was just an ordinary woman. How could she hope her love would overcome *that?*

''I'm sorry, Gideon,'' Jake said. ''I realized they were despicable and without conscience, but this—'' He raked his hands through his hair in a gesture much like the one his brother often made. ''I'm sorry to make you talk about it, but I had to know.''

''Yes, I understand. We might have shared a childhood, but you don't love me as Brooke does, so you have no reason to trust me now.''

Brooke bit down on her lower lip to keep her sob inside. Gideon accepted the lack of love in his life so matter-of-factly, it broke her heart.

''Will you let me go?'' Gideon asked.

''We still need to reach a deal,'' Jake replied. ''Under the circumstances, I'll recommend against any jail time.''

Brooke whirled on Jake. ''What's wrong with you? Don't you think he's suffered enough? He said he'll give you what you want.''

Gideon hooked his arm in front of her shoulders and pulled her back against his chest. ''It's all right, Brooke. We do need to bargain, because there are several things I want too.''

''I can't let you go until the Coalition is destroyed, Gideon,'' Jake said. ''You see that, don't you? Call it protective custody. Marcus, Faith and Gretchen understand the danger we're in. Even Connor, the brother who didn't grow up as part of Code Proteus, realizes he has to take precautions.''

''Good. I'm pleased you understand, because once the Coalition discovers I'm no longer under their control, they will stop at nothing to acquire another mind to use. You all must be protected.''

''We've been given the use of a private island off the coast of Portugal. Our brothers and our sisters have gathered there, along with their spouses and many of the people who have put their resources into fighting the Coalition. They'll remain safe on the other side of the world until the showdown with the Coalition is over.''

''That's what I want for Brooke,'' Gideon said. ''I won't help you unless I can be assured she's safe.''

''Done,'' Jake said. ''I'll arrange to have her flown out of here tomorrow.''

''Wait a minute.'' Brooke tried to turn but Gideon held her securely. ''I'm not leaving without you.''

''Second,'' Gideon continued, ''I want access to the police records in Kansas.''

Jake nodded. ''Would this be in regard to the arrest warrant for Brooke Pritchard?''

She went motionless. ''You knew?''

''He's my brother,'' Gideon said, not sounding the least surprised. ''If he learned I was seeing you, he would have researched every detail about you thoroughly. I want the charges dropped and the record expunged, Jake.''

''Agreed.'' Jake regarded Brooke. ''You might be interested to know that Frank Shomburg is presently serving time in a federal prison for tax evasion.''

She was grateful that Gideon was holding her. To have the fear that had haunted her disappear so quickly was enough to make her knees give out again. She grasped his arm, dropped her head back against his shoulder and shuddered.

''And third,'' Gideon said. ''I want privacy.''

Jake frowned. ''We can't—''

''This is not negotiable. Because you intervened in my plans before I could complete them, I must be separated from the woman I love so she will be safe, and I don't wish to say goodbye in front of my jailers.''

Jake glanced at Brooke. ''All right. We can find a way to accommodate you elsewhere while I arrange the flight.''

Brooke had no intention of leaving, whatever the two of them said. She was about to voice a protest when Gideon crossed his other arm over her chest and squeezed her tightly enough to steal her breath. ''Then we have a deal,'' he said. ''At dawn I will give you what you want, Jake, but the remainder of the night is mine.''

The house that Jake and the FBI had been using as their base of operations had once belonged to the manager of Redemption's pulp mill. It was located in what was known locally as Snob Hill, an enclave of elegant homes on the opposite side of town from the mill—and the mill's odors—and it was only a mile and a half down the highway from the turnoff to Redcom Systems. The building was custom-built, luxuriously furnished and very private, reaching three stories high on the east side of a knoll. In daylight there would be a magnificent view of the town and the valley from the windows that stretched across the front, but the sky was still black when the unmarked van pulled into the garage at the back of the house.

The transfer from the Redemption jail had been accomplished swiftly and in complete secrecy. As it turned out, the FBI had planned to move Gideon to their base before daybreak anyway to ensure that no one but the sheriff and Jake's team were aware that Gideon was Achilles, and that Achilles was in custody.

And it was clear that he was still in custody, whatever Jake wanted to call it, Brooke thought as she followed Jake and Gideon from the garage to the house. There might not be steel mesh on the windows here, but the place was filled with grim-faced men with neat haircuts and the telltale bulge of shoulder holsters under their conservative suits.

Jake led the way to a corridor on the ground floor. "This served as the housekeeper's suite," he said, stopping at a door halfway down the corridor. "It's a self-contained unit. I called ahead to have it prepared for you. I'll return tomorrow when we're ready to commence."

Gideon slipped his arm around Brooke and reached for the doorknob. "And you'll take care of my other two requests, Jake?"

"I always keep my word, Gideon." There was an edge to Jake's voice. "I hope you'll keep yours."

"I assume you'll be posting men at this door and outside the house to be sure I do."

"Yes. I'm sorry."

"If I were in your place, I would do the same."

The housekeeper's suite was spacious, decorated as luxuriously as the other parts of the house that Brooke had glimpsed on her way through. There was a sitting room, a bedroom and a ceramic-tiled bathroom with a sunken tub, all done in tasteful shades of cream and brick. Yet several items were obviously missing. There was no telephone or computer, no TV or sound system, not even a coffee maker or a clock. Every electronic device that could conceivably have been adapted into a communication apparatus had been removed. That must have been what Jake had meant about having the rooms prepared.

But Brooke hardly glanced at her surroundings. The moment Jake left them alone, she turned to Gideon. "I'm not going to be shipped off to some Portuguese island. You need me."

He didn't argue. He smiled and stroked her cheek. "You love me. That's why you say that."

Her nerves were strung so tightly, his gentle caress made her shiver. "It's not that I don't appreciate your concern. I do. I'm glad we're out of that jail. It was like a cage."

"There are many different types of cages, Brooke, but you're right, that was one of the worst."

"Oh, no. I'm sorry. I didn't mean to remind you about how those people—" She had to swallow hard to steady her voice. "Gideon, I don't know how you survived what they did to you without going crazy."

His mouth quirked. "I had plenty of doubts concerning my sanity, believe me." He grasped her hips and pulled her against him. "But I can think of better things to do with the four and a half hours before sunrise."

She pressed her hands to his chest. "Didn't you hear me before? I told you that I'm not leaving you and I mean it. Now more than ever, you shouldn't be alone. There wasn't any reason to make saying goodbye part of your deal with Jake."

"It's not the talking that I needed the privacy for," he murmured.

"Gideon—"

"It's the sex."

Damn, he'd done it again. Just when she thought she had a handle on the situation, he would do something that would turn her inside out. "Yes, that's probably what every one of those FBI men who are stationed outside this room are thinking, too."

He raised his eyebrows. "Of course, that's what they would think. It would be logical to conclude that a couple in love would have sex before they part."

Incredibly, despite the tension of the past few hours—or maybe because of it—she laughed. "Oh, Gideon. You really don't have one bit of self-consciousness."

He curled his fingers around her buttocks, lifting her so their lower bodies fit together. "I wouldn't let anything interfere with what I want. But it's not just sex, is it, Brooke? I should have called it making love, because it must be love that makes this urge I feel to join my body to yours so powerful."

Brooke caught her breath at the feel of him. He was already hard. She felt a surge of response tingle between her thighs.

"Even if we only join our hands, it steadies me and fills me with your warmth." He shifted to scoop her into his arms. Cradling her against his chest, he walked to the bedroom. "I would be content simply to hold you next to my heart and watch the stars fade as the sky lightens toward dawn, if that's all you want. As long as we're together."

She laid her head on his shoulder as he carried her through the doorway. "Being with you is like some carnival ride that keeps jerking me in different directions without any warning.''

''Do you like carnival rides?''

''Sometimes. When they don't scare me.''

''You don't need to be frightened of me, Brooke. I would never do anything to hurt you.''

''I know that. It's not you who frightens me, it's the situation.''

He put one knee on the mattress and leaned over to lay her in the center of the bed. ''I'm going to alter the situation, Brooke. I'm going to free myself and all of us from the threat of the Coalition.''

''I believe you, Gideon. You've never lied to me.''

''That's right. I haven't lied to you and I never will.'' He discarded his boots, then knelt on the bed, straddling her thighs as he unfastened the buttons of his shirt. ''You're my truth.''

He'd said that before, she realized, on New Year's Eve. It seemed so long ago now, but in reality only a little over a week had passed. She thought of something else he had said that night, when she'd asked him if he was married. There had been so many facts to take in, she hadn't fully thought out the implications of them all, but... ''Oh, my God,'' she said. ''You were telling the truth when you said there had never been another woman. That first night we made love really was your first time.''

''Yes.''

''I thought I had misunderstood you. I hadn't believed anyone could be so...good without practice.'' She brushed aside the edges of his shirt and ran her fingers over the firm ridges of his abdomen. ''You're amazing. How did you know what— I mean, you were isolated for years so how could you—''

''I have some reference books on the subject.''

She laughed softly and moved her hands to his thighs. ''Gideon, you really are a genius. And one hell of a fast learner.''

''And you, Brooke, are the best teacher.''

''I'm glad that I happened to be the one who—'' Another thought occurred to her. ''Gideon, the first time we made love, you thought you were going to die from that immune thing. That's why you went all weird when you realized that Rudy had bitten you.''

''Yes. I thought my immune reaction had been triggered and I had only a few useful hours left.''

She pulled her hands away. ''So you figured you had nothing left to lose and you didn't want to die a virgin? If some other woman had been around instead of me—''

He grabbed her hands and pressed them to his lips. ''Brooke, no.'' He kissed her palms. ''The wonder of our first night together wouldn't have happened with anyone but you. The bond between us goes beyond the physical. We're two halves of one whole. I hadn't understood that until you told me about your past. No other woman would have drawn me the way you do, and I don't believe you would have felt this connection with any other man. Even though we followed different paths to reach the point where our lives crossed, we were destined to find each other.''

''Gideon—''

''If some other man had been around that night in the parking lot and had helped you get away from

Rudy, you wouldn't have taken him to your bed, would you?''

''No, of course not. Another man wouldn't have believed he was going to—'' The full significance of what he'd done struck her all at once. She gasped. ''You helped me even though you believed that touching another person would kill you.''

He nodded. ''Yes. I had no regrets.''

How could she doubt the genuineness of his feelings? How could she be concerned with her own ego? He had been willing to die for her. Next to that, everything else seemed trivial. She shook her head. ''There's just so much to absorb. It's going to take me awhile.''

''I'm sorry we must still measure our time in hours.'' He leaned forward to catch the neckline of her sweater in his teeth. He tugged it downward until he could rub his nose over the upper curve of her breast.

She sighed in pleasure at the feel of his breath on her skin. She sifted her fingers through his hair. ''When this is over, when the Coalition is broken up and the criminals are in jail, what will we do then?''

''What do you want? Tell me and I will do everything within my power to make your wish come true.''

''You said you wanted me to leave Redemption with you. Do you still feel that way?''

He sat back on his heels to look at her, his gaze suddenly intent. ''I want to spend the rest of my life with you, Brooke. But more than that, I want the right to share your future.''

''The right? Gideon—''

"I can never make amends for the things I did as Achilles. Even if I destroy the evil I helped to create, I can't erase the effects of what I've done."

"But you believed you had no choice if you wanted to live." She lifted herself onto her elbows. "You were drugged, you were lied to, and you were an impressionable child when it started."

"It ends tomorrow, Brooke."

At his tone, she felt a chill. She looked at him more carefully. "Gideon, that sounds so final."

He cupped her face in his hands. "The first time we made love, I wished for three things. And then on New Year's Eve, I made the same wishes again."

She remembered his haunted expression, the rage in his gaze—that had been the night he had discovered the lie. She turned her head and brushed her lips across the edge of the gauze on his palm. The scope of what he'd endured staggered her. "What were they, Gideon?"

"I wished the night would never end. I wished we could stay like this forever." His eyes gleamed with a sheen of moisture. He leaned down and pressed his mouth to hers in a hard kiss, then moved his lips over her face, kissing everywhere he touched. "I still wish that, Brooke," he said. His voice was rough. "I know it's selfish, but I don't want morning to come. I want to fill every one of my senses with your essence and use my body to show you how I feel." He stretched on top of her and moved his lips to her ear. "And when our bodies are spent, I'll use my words. After that, my thoughts."

She returned her hands to his hair, feeling the thick

locks slide sensuously over her wrists. Her pirate with the soul of a poet. "And your third wish?"

He touched his forehead to hers. "I wished I were human."

Pain knifed through her heart. She pushed him to his side and placed her hand on his chest. She found the ridge of scar tissue with her fingers. "Whatever you were told, or whatever high-tech way you were conceived, you are human, Gideon. This proves it."

"Just because I can bleed—"

"I'm not talking about your DNA or what makes up the packaging." She thumped the place over his heart. "I mean what's inside."

"I don't know what's inside. I don't remember."

"You don't need to. I'm taking it on faith. Stop beating yourself up for things that weren't in your control. You got a raw deal. You made the best of it. Sure, you made mistakes. They were huge mistakes, but—" She caught his chin and brought her face to his. "But none of us are perfect, Gideon. We're all flawed. That's what makes us human."

He stared at her in silence. The only sounds in the room were their breathing and the rush of her pulse in her ears.

She traced his mouth with her fingertips. "Could we stop talking now? I can think of so many better things to do with the time—"

She never got the chance to finish her request. Gideon brought his mouth to hers in a kiss that left her straining for air. What had begun leisurely when he'd carried her into the bedroom took on a sense of necessity. They weren't gentle as they rid each other of their clothes. Their bodies responded as they always did, muscles quivering under each caress, hearts racing with eagerness, skin turning slick as they slid together.

Yet as Brooke crossed her ankles behind Gideon's back and lifted her hips to his thrusts, she knew something was different. Something had changed. There was an honesty here that went beyond the secrets she'd learned mere hours ago. She wasn't even sure she could call it love. It was more. It was a sense of belonging, of…coming home.

"I'm not leaving you, Gideon," she whispered. "You do know that, don't you?"

"Yes, Brooke. I know."

"So this isn't goodbye."

Only later would she realize that he hadn't replied.

Thirteen

It was difficult to tell whether the sun had risen. A warm front from the coast had drifted in overnight, leaving the valley cloaked in mist. Fine droplets condensed on the outer pane of the bedroom window and drizzled down the glass, carving shiny cracks in the solid wall of gray outside.

Brooke usually liked the fog. It was peaceful, like being enveloped in a cloud, but this morning the dim gray she saw when she first opened her eyes looked sinister. Shivering, she turned over and reached toward Gideon's warmth.

Her hand touched empty space. She ran her palm over the sheet. It still carried a trace of Gideon's body heat. The pillow bore an impression of where he'd rested his head. He couldn't have been gone long.

She sat up, expecting to hear the sound of running water, but there was nothing. No footsteps, no soft slide of a towel over skin. Gideon's clothes were no longer on the floor where she'd tossed them. There was no sign that anyone else was here.

She pulled his pillow to her breasts, inhaling the scent of his hair, not wanting to get up and break the spell of the night before. How could he be gone when she still felt so connected to him?

But deep inside she knew she was alone. She'd awakened alone too often not to recognize the feeling. She wrapped the sheet around her and padded to the bathroom. Of course, it was empty. Holding the sheet to her breasts, she ran to the sitting room.

The condensation on the outside of the window there had been smeared, as if someone had brushed against it. Her heart kicked into a stuttering rhythm as she crossed the room and looked outside.

How had he done it? There was a steep drop down the mountain on this side of the house. And she was positive that the FBI would be patrolling outside. How had he managed to slip away without being caught?

She pressed her hand to the window, straining to see through the fog. The chill from the glass seeped through her palm and up her arm. The shiver that shook her was from more than the cold.

It would be comforting to pretend he'd escaped because he wanted his freedom, that he was running away. She wouldn't have blamed him if he had. After being imprisoned by the Coalition's lies for his entire adult life, Gideon wouldn't feel that Jake's promise to recommend no jail time would be enough of a guarantee.

But during the brief negotiations of the night before, Gideon hadn't asked for any guarantees for himself, had he? He hadn't been interested in his freedom or his safety. He'd only bargained for Brooke's freedom and Brooke's safety...and for the chance to say goodbye.

"Gideon," she whispered. "What have you done?"

Yet she knew. The clues had been there all along.

He never lied. He had promised Jake would get what he wanted. He hadn't said how.

I'm going to free myself and all of us from the threat of the Coalition.

He'd said he had a program that only he could implement. Not once had he actually agreed to let Jake take over.

It ends tomorrow, Brooke.

Damn. *Damn!* Why hadn't she seen this sooner? She pushed away from the window and raced back to the bedroom. She threw on her clothes, trying to keep the tears at bay. She couldn't break down now. All right, even if her love wasn't enough to overcome the damage of his past, Gideon needed her. He still didn't realize that he didn't have to be alone, he didn't have to do this himself, he didn't have to prove anything....

I can never make amends for the things I did as Achilles. Even if I destroy the evil I helped to create, I can't erase the effects of what I've done.

He hadn't talked about a future with her. Instead, he'd spoken of not deserving one.

He wasn't running away. He was going *back.* To destroy the Coalition, whatever the cost. He intended to sacrifice himself if necessary so that—

"No!" she cried, running to the door. She tried the knob. It wouldn't turn—they must have locked it from the outside. She pounded on the panels hard enough to make her fists sting. "Help! Let me out!"

The door was opened by one of the FBI agents she'd met at the jail. She tried to push past him but he grabbed her arm. "Miss Carter, you can't—"

''Let go of me, Lansky.'' She twisted, trying to break free. ''I need to see Jake Ingram. Now.''

''You can't. He's busy.''

''Gideon's in danger. Jake has to stop—'' She jerked, seizing on one last desperate shred of hope. ''Do you mean he's already begun working with Gideon? Did you let Gideon go past? Where is he?''

Lansky didn't reply. Without loosening his grip on her, he gestured to two other men who were stationed at the end of the corridor. They entered the housekeeper's suite. Less than a minute later, they returned, shaking their heads. Lansky took a cell phone from the pocket of his jacket and hit a button with his thumb. ''Ingram was right,'' he said into the phone. ''We can confirm that Achilles is on the move.''

The fog was Gideon's ally. A lucky break. It had concealed his slow descent down the slope from the house. It had muffled the noise of the crash as he'd lost his footing and tumbled the final ten feet. He was grateful for the cover it provided as he made his way through the forest.

Yet the concealment worked both ways. The landmarks he had used to guide his path before were virtually invisible. Over the past several minutes, the fog had begun to thin, but Gideon still had to move more slowly than he wished to ensure he was maintaining the right heading. How much time did he have left?

It made no difference. He was going to complete his task whether he had hours or only minutes. Whatever it took.

The first night Gideon had left the compound, he'd

wondered how deep the evil ran in his soul. This was the only hope he had of learning the answer.

"That's far enough, Gideon."

At the voice, he froze. The fog distorted the sound, making it difficult to pinpoint the location of the speaker. But he knew instantly who had spoken. He peered into the murk around him, noting the dark outline of tree trunks to his left and the glistening bulk of a boulder to his right.

He focused on the trees. "Jake?"

A tall form materialized from the gloom. "A little damp for a walk, little brother, wouldn't you say?"

Gideon hadn't been aware that he was being followed; obviously the fog had given Jake the same advantage it had given him. "What do you want?"

"I reasoned that you were going to try to leave. That's why I left instructions to make it easy for you."

"Why?"

"I've been tracking you since you left the house because I needed to see which direction you would take. This isn't the route to the highway out of town, Gideon. This is the way to that tunnel you've been using to get in and out of the compound."

"Yes. I imagine that would be obvious by now."

"I'm glad to see that my faith in you wasn't misplaced. You haven't changed after all. The Gideon I knew would have tried to do the same thing."

"Would he? I have no way of knowing."

Jake moved closer. His hair was damp from the fog, his features pinched. Was it from irritation, or from concern? "You always were stubborn."

"I told you I'd give you what you wanted at dawn. I'm going to destroy the Coalition."

"Not on your own. I didn't agree to that. You were to give me the program and let me implement it."

"You can't."

"Why not?"

Gideon regarded his brother carefully. Jake appeared empty-handed but he was probably armed. "You still don't trust me," he said.

"It isn't a matter of trust. I've already requested that the charges against you be dropped, Gideon. I set the process into motion during the night."

He hadn't expected this. It cleared one obstacle to his future, but the most serious one remained. "None of us will be free until the Coalition is stopped."

"You're not the only one who has a score to settle with Croft and Payne and Grimble. I want them stopped just as much as you do. I have the same abilities."

"The program is on a disk in my quarters. It can't be implemented from outside the Coalition compound."

"I can hack into it."

"Not the mainframe I designed," Gideon said. "The compound is underground, shielded by tons of rock on top of a layer of lead sheeting so that no remote signal can penetrate. The land line we use for networking with outside computers is protected by a one-way trap-door function I developed that is unbreachable. The programming must be done from within the compound. I'm the only one who knows the layout. Therefore, I'm the one who must implement it.''

Jake stepped in front of him. ''I can't let you return to the compound. The risk to your safety is too great.''

Gideon assessed his brother, trying to decide whether or not he could overpower him. With his right hand injured, he couldn't be certain of winning a physical confrontation, so he would have to consider force only a last resort. ''Leave now, Jake. Tell them you couldn't find me.''

''You really don't remember me, do you?'' Jake asked. ''Otherwise, you'd never suggest that.''

''I remember that you didn't like to lose.''

Jake muttered a curse and walked to the boulder. He kicked at some moss-covered rocks near the base. ''Mark gave you your nickname. Do you remember that?''

Gideon shook his head.

''He thought it was a joke, naming you after a legendary warrior. You hated to fight.''

''I'm not that child anymore. Too many years have passed.''

Jake took off his glove to rub his face. ''Gideon, I'm sorry for the years the Coalition held you. Brooke was right. The rest of us had normal lives and a shot at happiness, but you never had a chance. I called them this morning.''

''Who?''

''The rest of the family. They're all eager to see you and welcome you back. They want to make up for the love the Coalition cheated you of. You don't need to do this.''

Gideon felt a pang of longing. Family. It was difficult to adjust. First Brooke, now his siblings. "Did you tell them what I am? What I've done?"

"They already knew. It doesn't make any difference."

Gideon looked away. He didn't want Jake to see how much he wanted to believe him.

But somehow, Jake guessed anyway. "That's it, isn't it?" he asked. "You're not doing this out of justice or revenge or stubbornness. You're doing this for redemption."

"It's getting late," Gideon said, starting forward.

Jake blocked his path. "That's the real reason you're determined to go after the Coalition alone. You think you need to make up for what you've done. You think you don't deserve to be loved."

"I am loved. Brooke loves me."

"Then why are you throwing her love away?"

Gideon had no reply. Damn, he wasn't accustomed to dealing with a genius.

"Because that's what you're doing," Jake said. "Those years with the Coalition made you question what you were, so you decided you need to prove it."

Gideon glanced around. The fog was continuing to thin. The sun's rays were penetrating the forest, turning the moisture in the air into a white veil. How much time had he wasted? "Every minute I delay lessens my chances of getting into the compound undetected. Move aside, Jake."

"No. Go back to the house, Gideon."

"No."

Jake slipped his hand into his coat. "I'd hoped I wouldn't need to do this."

Gideon readied himself to grab for the gun, but rather than withdrawing a weapon, Jake withdrew a small notebook.

"These are some of our father's notes," Jake said. "Gretchen spent months decoding them. It details everything about Code Proteus."

"The project is over, Jake. It no longer matters."

"It does matter. The past explains the present."

The words were familiar. Gideon realized he'd once said them himself to Brooke.

"It would have been best to let your memories return naturally," Jake continued. "But there's no time."

"You're right. There isn't time for any of this. I don't want to fight you, but—"

"'There was a crooked man who walked a crooked mile.'"

Gideon felt as if he'd been punched in the stomach. He couldn't catch his breath. He stared at Jake.

His brother's voice melted into someone else's. The scent of the forest became the bitter tang of chemicals.

Someone was reciting a rhyme. He didn't like it. He wanted them to stop but his lips were forming the words along with them....

"'He found a crooked sixpence upon a crooked stile.'"

It was nonsense. The phrases were meaningless, nothing but a child's poem, but they made Gideon begin to shake. He staggered backward, stumbling on a rotting log. He slapped his hand against a hemlock tree to regain his balance.

Jake followed him. He was still speaking, but his words seemed to be coming from a distance, spiraling through time. "'He bought a crooked cat.'"

More pieces were tearing loose inside, ripping away from the barrier over his past. The house on the beach. The children. His mother applauding as Gideon showed her what he'd made. His father lifting him onto his shoulders to give him a ride.

"'Who caught a crooked mouse...'"

Gideon looked at Jake. Was it an illusion from the fog? The image of his brother was wavering. He could see the boy in the man, the older brother he'd idolized.

"'And they all lived together...'"

The words were sparking in his mind. They were the last secret. The hidden code that was his alone. They had been imbedded so deeply, he hadn't known they were there, but now they were whirling to the surface. The fog was thinning. He could see them, feel them, hear the child's voice as he repeated the verse....

There was a crooked man, who walked a crooked mile,

He found a crooked sixpence upon a crooked stile.

He bought a crooked cat who caught a crooked mouse,

And they all lived together in a little crooked house.

As soon as he completed the rhyme, the rest of the memories that had been imprisoned burst free. Gideon keeled over, bracing his hands on his knees to keep from falling. The images flowed past in a dizzying blur.

Uncle Oliver and Aunt Agnes's laboratory. The needles. The tests.

The playroom filled with scale models and chalkboards, the weekly shipment of new toys, the joy of learning, of feeling his brain work.

The trips into town to the library, the school, the movies. The good-night hugs and kisses.

Jake squeezed his shoulder. "I'm sorry, Gideon. I realize it's a shock but I had to make you remember before you threw it away."

Gideon gulped for air. He lifted his head. "I want to see them."

"Who?"

"Mark, Grace and Faith. You said they're all right. I have to see—"

Another memory surged up, blotting out the others. His father's funeral. His mother's face, looking grim and determined as she tried to pull Gideon out of bed. He hadn't recognized her. His memory had been blocked and he'd fought her. Then there'd been a sharp crack. Pain and blood. And his mother's face crumpled in grief, in loss, in such unutterable sadness....

Gideon straightened and clasped Jake's arm. "Where's Mom?"

"She died last year."

Sunshine broke through the boughs overhead. The fog was dissipating, revealing more with each second that passed. Loss and pain. Love and hope. The bad along with the good. "She tried to save us," Gideon said. "I remember."

"She did save us, Gideon. Because, before she died, she made sure we would all find each other again."

"And thereby find ourselves."

Jake's eyes shone. "Yes. And find ourselves."

Gideon felt a sharp pain in his chest. It was his heart expanding.

And that was when Gideon finally remembered the love.

He'd thought he'd never known that emotion before Brooke, but it had been there all along. It was the base on which all the other memories were built. It was what had given him the inner strength to endure the cruelty of the Coalition for over twenty years without losing himself.

He yanked Jake's arm, pulling him into a firm embrace. "It's good to see you, Jake. You look so much like Dad."

Jake clapped him on the back. "And as usual, you need a haircut."

Gideon blinked hard. "You haven't changed. You're still trying to boss me around."

"That's because I still know best." He pulled back, grabbed Gideon's shoulders and looked at him. "You don't need to prove anything to the people who love you. Turn around, Gideon. Go back to the house."

He was still reeling from the return of his memories, so it took him a moment to understand what Jake was talking about. He shook his head. "Bringing back my memories doesn't make me change my mind. The programming has to be done from inside the compound. I told you, this is the only way.''

''Wrong. Because the Coalition had you all those years, they didn't try too hard to find the rest of us. You don't owe us, we owe you. It's time to let someone else take over the fight.''

''Jake—''

''I'm sorry, but you know how I hate to lose.'' Jake released his grip on Gideon's shoulders and twisted as if he were turning away, then swung back suddenly before Gideon had a chance to react.

Jake's fist caught him square on the jaw, knocking him backward into the hemlock. Gideon's head hit the trunk, the forest spun, the ground rushed upward. And Gideon's world once more dissolved into a wall of gray.

Brooke stood on the terrace at the side of the house. Despite the sunshine that poured down on the stone slabs beneath her boots, her feet were numb. Her báck was aching. Lansky had brought her a mug of coffee twenty minutes ago, but she had let it grow cold in her hands. She didn't want to move. She didn't want to take her gaze from the trees at the base of the knoll.

Jake would find him and stop him, wouldn't he? If anyone could convince Gideon to change his mind, it would be his brother, wouldn't it? They shared the same genes, the same genius. Jake wouldn't let Gideon risk his life and his sanity by walking back into that group of...

She couldn't think of a word that was vile enough

to describe the Coalition. *They* were the ones who weren't human.

"Please, Gideon," she whispered. "Please, come back to me."

She had said it so many times, imagined seeing him so often, at first she didn't realize that the movement in the shadows was real. She held her breath and walked to the railing at the edge of the terrace.

A man strode out from beneath the canopy of boughs and started toward the slope that led to the house. He was too distant for her to make out his features. That didn't stop Brooke. The mug dropped from her hands and shattered on the stones as she vaulted the railing. "Gideon!"

Her cry was snatched away by the wind. The man didn't look up.

Brooke found the path that led downward. She started to run. Pebbles and moss slid beneath her boots. She dug in her heels to control her descent but she didn't slow down. Her heart was pounding so hard in her throat, she couldn't swallow. She lost sight of him as she skidded into a bush and she whimpered. Had it been her imagination? Was he real?

She rounded the bush and suddenly there he was on the path in front of her.

His hair had come loose. It whipped back from his face in the wind. There was dried blood on the side of his temple and a swelling bruise on his chin. His jaw was set into a hard line, his fists clenched.

Brooke slid to a stop. He looked different. It wasn't just the blood and the bruise. His expression was grim, yet there was a new lightness to him, as if the shadows had been chased away....

It struck her then. It was the sunshine. This was the first time she'd ever seen him in broad daylight.

"Gideon?"

He opened his arms.

She launched herself at him, no longer trying to hold back her tears. Only when she felt the familiar warmth of his embrace did she breathe freely once more. "Are you all right? You're bleeding."

"I'm fine, Brooke." He pressed his face to her hair. "You're beautiful in the sunlight. Let's make sure our house has plenty of windows."

"Our house?"

He kissed her. It was fast but thorough, a silent promise of what was yet to come. Then he looped his arm behind her waist and guided her back up the path. "There are so many plans I want to make with you, Brooke. First, I think we should get married."

She stumbled, catching his hand to keep from falling. "Married?"

"It's the logical next step for two people in love, especially if we have children."

Why did she want to laugh? Only Gideon would propose like this. She bit her lip and nodded. "Okay."

"Jake gave me my shot at happiness and I'm not letting it slip away."

She glanced behind them. "Where is he? Did he find you?"

"He found me. He knocked me out and took my place."

"What?"

"He's gone into the compound to finish what I started. I need to alert his men to stand by. Damn, if I didn't love him, I'd probably wring his neck for playing hero that way."

Brooke stopped and grabbed Gideon's coat. She focused on his face. It was more than the sunshine that had driven away the shadows. The radiance in his gaze came from within. "Gideon, something else happened. I can see it. What—"

"I remember. Everything. My past, my family, myself. All of it." He smiled. "I know what I am, Brooke."

She had to wipe her eyes so she could see him clearly. His smile was unlike any she'd seen before. The lost-child loneliness was gone. In its place was...peace.

She touched her fingers to his bruised jaw. "And what are you, Gideon?"

"I'm a man who has been blessed. With family. With love and the promise of a future." He grasped her waist and lifted her so his gaze was level with hers. "I had thought the proof of my love would be my willingness to die."

She'd known that. It was what had driven her half-crazy all morning while she'd waited.

"But I was wrong, Brooke," he said. "The truth is, love gives us a reason to live."

* * * * *

There are more secrets to reveal—
don't miss out!
Coming in May 2004 to
Silhouette Books

When Jake Ingram is taken captive by
the Coalition, a sexy undercover agent is
sent to brainwash him. Though he finds
her hard to resist, can he trust this
mysterious beauty?

CHECK MATE

by

Beverly Barton

FAMILY SECRETS: *Five extraordinary*
siblings. One dangerous past.
Unlimited potential.

And now, for a sneak peek,
just turn the page...

One

Much to his surprise, Jake actually slept several hours before waking with a cramp in his arm. When he first awoke, he tugged on his wrist and couldn't figure out why it was handcuffed to the bed, but then reality hit him like a splash of ice-cold water. Everything came back in an instant flash. His beating, capture and transport to this isolated mountain cabin. Using his free hand, he massaged his aching arm; then as he flipped over, he glanced at the person lying in the bed next to him. Dr. Mariah Brooks. The woman fascinated him, but he didn't have the luxury of fully exploring that fascination. What he needed from her— and needed as soon as possible—was her help in escaping. Accomplishing that goal would take finesse on his part. If he pushed too hard, too fast, she might balk. But then again, he really couldn't wait.

He wondered how deeply involved she was with the Coalition, how many years she'd been working for them. Was she doing it for the money or was she committed to their cause? If it was money, he could offer her twice what they were paying her. If it was a true commitment on her part, then he might be screwed, unless he could charm her into helping him, regardless of her loyalty to an unjust cause. Women had been known to betray their families, their countries, their own valued principles, all for love. Could he seduce Mariah into thinking she was in love with him? He didn't have much time. He needed to put a plan into motion immediately.

"Dr. Brooks?" Jake called her name softly, and when she didn't respond, he said it a bit louder. He could barely make out her dark form moving beneath the covers, but when she turned over, he felt certain she was looking his way.

"Is something wrong?" she asked, her voice sleep-husky.

"I've got a cramp in my arm," he admitted hoarsely. "Would you mind removing the handcuff for a few minutes?"

"All right." As soon as she rolled out of bed, she flipped on the bedside lamp, lighting the room with a forty-watt creamy-white glow.

He watched her as she got to her feet—long slender feet, with red toenails. Red toenails! Now wasn't that interesting? Dr. Brooks's fingernails were short and sported clear polish. Neat, professional, boring. But her toenails were fire-engine red. Bright, sexy, ultra-feminine. And exciting.

She retrieved the key for the handcuffs, then approached the bed. He looked up at her and smiled. "Did anyone ever tell you that you're awfully pretty when you first wake up?"

Narrowing her gaze to slits, she glowered at him as she reached down, unlocked the handcuffs, removed one cuff from the bedpost and then pulled the other cuff from his wrist. He dropped his arm and sighed dramatically while he rubbed his arm from wrist to elbow.

''I don't know what sort of game you think you're playing,'' she said, ''but I advise you to forget it.''

As she turned to walk away, he reached out, grabbed her arm and dragged her down until she toppled over on top of him. He wasn't quite sure what to expect, didn't know if she'd slap him, just jump up to get away from him or verbally reprimand him again. She surprised him by sliding off him and onto her side, then she stared deeply into his eyes. Those sky-blue eyes of hers appeared twice as bright, twice as sparkling, against the golden glow of her dark complexion. In that one instant of complete stillness, Jake slid his arm around her. She didn't move, didn't respond, and he realized she was holding her breath.

He caressed her neck with his fingertips. ''Do you play chess, Mariah?''

She shook her head, tossing her thick black hair ever so slightly from side to side. ''I jog, I play tennis, I work out at the gym. As far as games go, I haven't played any since I was a kid. Checkers and jacks were my favorites.''

He continued caressing her, allowing his fingers to linger over her earlobe a few minutes before forking them through her hair. ''In chess, each player's goal is to attack the enemy's king in such a way that the king can't escape. It's a game of wits. You must learn not only to evaluate your own moves, but to anticipate your opponent's next move.''

''Does chess have anything to do with the game you're trying to play with me?'' A shiver rippled through her when he cupped the back of her head and brought his mouth within a hairbreadth of hers.

"What do you think?"

"I think you should release me and go back to sleep. I plan to start our first session fairly early in the morning."

"Why don't we start now?" Before she had a chance to respond, he lowered his mouth and kissed her. Gently. Sweetly. Being careful not to seem too aggressive. For a split second she responded, giving herself over to the moment, but then she ended things. Abruptly. Withdrawing quickly, she stared at him, a startled expression widening her eyes.

"No." She uttered that one word before she pulled out of his arms and shot up off the bed. After turning from him, her back ramrod straight, she stood in place for several seconds before she faced him again. Without saying anything else, she grabbed his arm, manacled his wrist and yanked the cuffed hand high enough to secure the other hand to the bedpost.

Jake looked up at her, but she wouldn't meet his gaze. He'd had her there for a few seconds. She'd been his completely. Perhaps he'd been too gentle. Next time—and there would be a next time—he'd take her hard and fast, without giving her a chance to think.

"Should I apologize?" he asked.

Instead of responding, she turned and walked away, straight back to her bed. She dropped the key into her boot, which rested on the floor beside the bed. He watched her while she crawled beneath the covers and then switched off the lamp.

"Mariah?"

Silence.

"I don't like it any more than you do, you know," he told her. "How do you think I feel being attracted to a woman who plans to try to reactivate Oliver Grimble's programming embedded in my brain? Believe me, lady, you're the last woman on earth I want getting me hot and bothered." Say something, damn it, Jake thought. Had he really blown it with Mariah? Had the kiss been too much too soon? "We can't help it. Neither of us. I want you. You want me. It's that simple. We'll have to find a way to deal with it."

"Go to sleep, Jake," she said finally, her voice low and calm. "You need your rest."

"Avoiding talking about it isn't going to change anything. It's not going to make us want each other any less."

"Shut up, will you?"

Smiling, Jake burrowed his head into the fluffy pillow. He had her rattled. He considered his options and decided that keeping quiet was the wisest course of action right now. Mariah was interested, but she was no pushover. She would fight him every inch of the way. And if he knew women—and he did—she'd be cool and aloof come morning. He expected her to give him the cold shoulder and probably take a bit of perverse delight in trying to break down his defenses. His gut instincts told him that Dr. Mariah Brooks was accustomed to being the one in charge. Maybe he should let her believe she could control him, then, when she least expected it, make his move.

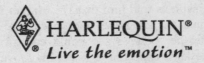

Five extraordinary siblings.

One dangerous past.

Unlimited potential.

If you missed the first riveting stories from Family Secrets, here's a chance to order your copies today!

0-373-61368-7	ENEMY MIND by Maggie Shayne	___ $4.99 U.S.	___ $5.99 CAN.
0-373-61369-5	PYRAMID OF LIES by Anne Marie Winston	___ $4.99 U.S.	___ $5.99 CAN.
0-373-61370-9	THE PLAYER by Evelyn Vaughn	___ $4.99 U.S.	___ $5.99 CAN.
0-373-61371-7	THE BLUEWATER AFFAIR by Cindy Gerard	___ $4.99 U.S.	___ $5.99 CAN.
0-373-61372-5	HER BEAUTIFUL ASSASSIN by Virginia Kantra	___ $4.99 U.S.	___ $5.99 CAN.
0-373-61373-3	A VERDICT OF LOVE by Jenna Mills	___ $4.99 U.S.	___ $5.99 CAN.
0-373-61374-1	THE BILLIONAIRE DRIFTER by Beverly Bird	___ $4.99 U.S.	___ $5.99 CAN.
0-373-61375-X	FEVER by Linda Winstead Jones	___ $4.99 U.S.	___ $5.99 CAN.
0-373-61376-8	BLIND ATTRACTION by Myrna Mackenzie	___ $4.99 U.S.	___ $5.99 CAN.
0-373-61377-6	THE PARKER PROJECT by Joan Elliot Pickart	___ $4.99 U.S.	___ $5.99 CAN.

(limited quantities available)

TOTAL AMOUNT $_____
POSTAGE & HANDLING $_____
($1.00 for one book; 50¢ for each additional)
APPLICABLE TAXES* $_____
<u>TOTAL PAYABLE</u> $_____
(Check or money order—please do not send cash)

To order, complete this form and send it, along with a check or money order for the total above, payable to **Family Secrets,** to:
In the U.S.: 3010 Walden Avenue, P.O. Box 9077, Buffalo, NY 14269-9077;
In Canada: P.O. Box 636, Fort Erie, Ontario L2A 5X3

Name:_____
Address:_____ City:_____
State/Prov.:_____ Zip/Postal Code:_____
Account # (if applicable):_____
075 CSAS

*New York residents remit applicable sales taxes.
*Canadian residents remit applicable GST and provincial taxes.

Visit us at www.silhouettefamilysecrets.com

FSBACK10

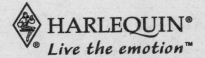

Silhouette®
Where love comes alive™

FAMILY SECRETS

Five extraordinary siblings.
One dangerous past.
Unlimited potential.

**Collect four (4) original proofs of purchase from
the back pages of four (4) Family Secrets titles
and receive a specialty themed free gift
valued at over $20.00 U.S.!**

Just complete the order form and send it, along with four (4) proofs of
purchase from four (4) different Family Secrets titles to: Family Secrets, P.O. Box
9047, Buffalo, NY 14269-9047, or P.O. Box 613, Fort Erie, Ontario L2A 5X3.

Name (PLEASE PRINT)

Address   Apt. #

City   State/Prov.   Zip/Postal Code

Please specify which themed gift package(s)
you would like to receive:

❏ PASSION DT5N
❏ HOME AND FAMILY DT5P
❏ TENDER AND LIGHTHEARTED DT5Q

❏ Have you enclosed your proofs of purchase?

Forrester Square
LEGACIES . LIES . LOVE .

Coming in April 2004…
a brand-new Forrester Square tale!

ILLEGALLY YOURS

by favorite
Harlequin American Romance® author

JACQUELINE DIAMOND

Determined to stay in America despite an
expired visa, pregnant Kara Tamaki turned to
attorney Daniel Adler for help. Daniel wasn't an
immigration lawyer, but he knew how to help
Kara stay in America—marry her!

Forrester Square…Legacies. Lies. Love.

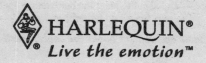

HARLEQUIN®
Live the emotion™

**Visit the Forrester Square Web site at
www.forrestersquare.com!**

FSQIY

Head to the wild and romantic West with...

USA TODAY bestselling authors

SUSAN MALLERY
CAIT LONDON

Lassoed Hearts

The ranching single dads in these two full-length novels are rugged, rough-edged—and about to meet the only women special enough to rope them into fatherhood...again!

Available everywhere books are sold in April 2004.